DRIVE

ALSO BY DIANA WIELER

THE RANVAN TRILOGY
    RANVAN: THE DEFENDER
    RANVAN: A WORTHY OPPONENT
    RANVAN: MAGIC NATION

BAD BOY
LAST CHANCE SUMMER

DRIVE
DIANA WIELER

A GROUNDWOOD BOOK

DOUGLAS & McINTYRE

TORONTO VANCOUVER BUFFALO

Groundwood Books/Douglas & McIntyre
585 Bloor Street West
Toronto, Ontario M6G 1K5

Distributed in the USA by Publishers Group West
1700 Fourth Street
Berkeley, CA 94710

We acknowledge the financial support of the Canada Council
for the Arts, the Ontario Arts Council and the Government of
Canada through the Book Publishing Industry Development
Program for our publishing activities.

Library of Congress data is available

Canadian Cataloguing in Publication Data
Wieler, Diana J. (Diana Jean)
Drive
A Groundwood book.
ISBN 0-88899-347-1 (bound) ISBN 0-88899-348-X (pbk.)
I. Title.
PS8595.I53143D74 1998   jC813'.54   C98-931363-8
PZ7.W54Dr 1998

Design by Michael Solomon
Cover illustration by Julia Bell
Printed and bound in Canada by Webcom

For Mellie and George,
who taught my sister and me
to dream out loud.

ONE

"Hi! How are you today?"

The couple studying the sedan turned abruptly, surprised to see me. I didn't really mean to sneak up on them, but most people don't like salesmen. If they see you coming they'll drift away. Pretty fast.

"We're just looking, thanks," the man said, shifting so that his shoulder was to me.

"Well, good. Because I'm not selling today," I said.

The woman looked up, puzzled. "Why not?"

I gestured around at the lot filled with new cars that glinted in the sun. "I don't work on nice days. It's too...nice."

She smiled. She was younger than the man, with reddish lights in her auburn hair. Maybe she was his second wife.

"Must be tough to earn a living, then," the man said, still not looking at me. "We've had the warmest winter in fifty years."

He was right. It was the middle of March and the snow was completely gone. I'd only been working at Five Star Ford for seven months, but I'd lived through the leanest winter in the dealership's history. We'd had rain in February, a miracle.

"It's a disaster," my sales manager had said. "Their damn cars keep starting. Half of us could have stayed in bed last month."

I wasn't someone who stayed in bed. My hand was already in my suit jacket pocket, fumbling for business cards.

"I'm Jens Friesen." I swept out a card to each of them with the slightest tilt of a bow. I'd always thought I did that bit well. "Are you looking for something like your current vehicle?" I nodded at the sporty import I'd seen them drive up in. It wasn't a two-seater but it might as well have been, for all the room there was in the back.

"I think we're interested in a *family* car," the woman said. The man gave her a look, but I felt a light go on inside me.

"Then you're really going to love the safety features of this model," I said cheerfully, pulling open the driver's door. "*Car and Driver* rated it the best mid-size choice for families with small children."

I had done my homework. Most evenings that winter I'd spent in my furnished suite, poring over the brochures and even the owner's manuals of the cars and trucks on our lot. I brought home magazines from the dealership, trying to memorize the ratings. It was easy to concentrate. I didn't have a television.

The woman was standing next to me, listening intently. I could smell her perfume – flowers and maybe spice.

"Now, the manufacturer is very concerned about the effect of air bags on children under forty pounds," I was saying.

"We don't have children yet," the man cut me off.

I felt a clutch of panic.

"You...you're really going to love the built-in safety bracket," I said quickly, opening the back door and climbing in. "A baby seat can hook right in."

The woman got in on the other side to see what I was talking about. I tried to keep my left elbow against me to hold my jacket closed. I had a stain on that shirt.

We found the bracket, a thin outcrop of metal at the back of the seat.

"It's a great idea," she said. "How does it work?"

I was eighteen years old. I'd never handled a baby seat, in this car or any other.

"You know, this is really premature," the man said suddenly. "And I have to get back to the office, honey."

"It's got to slide in somehow," I blurted.

The man was already walking away. The woman sighed and got out. I stood up, too, my heart sinking.

"Well, I appreciate your time, and if there's ever anything I can do —"

"I've got it," she said, holding up my business card as she backed away. She shrugged, a little sadly. "I'll come back when..."

I needed her to get pregnant now. This afternoon.

"I'm here all the time. Or they'll page me," I called. I watched them drive away in their sleek little car, too expensive to be loud. I'd forgotten to tell him what a great trade-in it would make. I'd forgotten to shake his hand.

It was Friday morning. The lot was dead. I walked back into the showroom.

Five Star Ford wasn't the biggest dealership in Winnipeg, but it was the one with fame attached. It was owned by Jack Lahanni, a running back who'd spent sixteen seasons in the CFL. There was a big picture of him hanging on the wall in the showroom, up high so you could see it over the cars on display. Fifty pounds and twenty years were on Jack Lahanni. In the picture he was wearing a crisp gray suit, but when I looked at it I still saw him in a green-and-white uniform, number 39. He had two Grey Cup championships and the league record for receptions in a single game. He was the second-greatest man I'd ever met.

Jack Lahanni wasn't the one who trained me. That was left to the sales manager, Sy Sudermann. I liked Sy. He was about fifty, with a square face that drooped at the corners and red highlights on his nose and cheeks. He still had a lot of thick black hair and he was proud of it. Someone had once told him he looked like Elvis and I think he believed it. He wore his sideburns longer than anyone else.

Before he'd been a sales manager, Sy had sold Cadillacs and other luxury cars.

"We had great margins in those days, Jens," he told me wistfully. "The late seventies, the early eighties – those were the golden years. There was so much margin built into a car that you'd earn three hundred bucks on a single caddy. And our lot had a bonus for a hat trick – if you sold three cars in a day, you got an extra hundred and fifty. You could actually have a thousand-dollar day."

I was a million miles from a thousand-dollar

day. I'd been selling about three vehicles a month, and margins were half what they were in the golden years. Then came February. So far, March hadn't been any better.

When I walked into the showroom, the door to Sy's office was closed. He was probably getting ready for the sales meeting we had every Friday at four o'clock. Just thinking about it pulled my stomach tight. I needed something to happen before then.

"Hey, Jens," Dave called, standing up at his desk, "looks like you almost had a live one."

"She's coming back," I said.

"When?"

"When she has a baby," I shrugged.

"Good God, man. And you didn't *volunteer*?"

Dave could make anyone laugh. He was older than me, in his twenties, but he still lived at home. He had three suits and a dozen ties, and he was the last one to run out of money when we went to the bar. February hadn't worried him at all.

It had worried Paul. He was the oldest of the six salesmen, with a wife and kids. The rest of us had stayed inside that month, telling stories but watching the lot. We kept our coats at our desks, ready. Paul spent his time on the phone, calling back every customer who'd ever bought a vehicle from him. It must have worked because even that February he was able to earn more than his draw. And the first Saturday in March, when Five Star Ford took out its regular ad in the newspaper, Paul's picture was up in the corner box, Sales Leader of the Month. Again.

The Winnipeg *Free Press* is shipped to all the small towns in the province. I knew my parents picked it up at the Lucky Mart in our home town of Ile-des-Sapins, not every day but always the Saturday edition. I would have given anything for my father to open the newspaper and see me in it.

I think I look like him. Friesen is a German name, and those genes gave me a square jaw and solid bones, shoulders made for lifting things. A girl at my high school in Rosetown once said I had a peasant's body, and even though I stopped liking her in that moment, it seemed to stick in my mind. My hair is that middle ash color that only turns really blond in the summer now, but it was nearly white until I was three years old.

My father named me Jens after his father, and I was proud of it, even though it's the kind of name other kids like to torture you with. But I didn't have my first fight until grade two, when Shane Lasko said my brother was retarded.

Daniel is two and a half years younger than

me, and he looks more like Mom. She's very French; before she married Dad her name was Desrochers. Mom and Daniel have the same huge brown eyes and dark hair, but on him the slender build came out wiry. To me he's all arms and legs, sinew and veins that seem to be just below the surface of his skin.

Growing up, we looked so different from one another.

"One for each of you," people told my parents, as if we were two flavors of ice cream — one Tiger-Tiger and one Rocky Road. Behind our backs I know they said other things, because Daniel didn't talk until he was four years old. In a small town, everyone is someone. My brother was the kid everybody thought was deaf, or worse.

My father, Karl Friesen, is the window man, the small-job renovation man. For awhile he had a guy working for him, Don Shibote, and that was when he had "Friesen Glass" painted on the side of the truck. I know he was proud of that. I remember how his voice seemed to deepen when he told a customer on the phone that he'd send his man out for the quote.

Just before I turned eighteen my father had a heart attack. In my mind that's when he really needed somebody helping him. But he didn't have disability insurance, so he didn't have the money and he had to let Don Shibote go. Dad didn't work for eight months. And somehow when he did, he wasn't Friesen Glass, he was just the window man again.

That's when I left home and moved to Winnipeg to work at Five Star Ford. Up until then, all I'd ever sold was chocolate-covered almonds, to raise money for my high-school football team, the Rosetown Raiders. But I believed that if I really wanted something, I could get it. If I just kept trying, if I didn't give up. When I left Rosetown Senior High, my picture was in the sports trophy case next to the office. Jens Friesen, Number 56, Most Improved Player and Chocolate King.

Over two seasons I had sold 3,364 boxes of those damn almonds.

◆

Judi the receptionist was on the phone but I saw her glance up, at the lot. I was out the showroom door before Dave could get up from his desk.

Don't run, Jens, I told myself. Don't blow it.

Halfway across the lot my heart was still thumping but I was walking casually, breathing easy.

The prospect was in his thirties, with close-cropped curly hair already starting to gray and a tan he couldn't have gotten in this part of the country, miracle spring or not. His suit had a faint expensive sheen like the ones Jack Lahanni wore. He was looking at what I called the power cars.

"Hi, how are you today?"

"Pretty good. The weather's beautiful."

I gestured at the shiny new cars. "And just look at the scenery."

He laughed. It was starting to feel like a great day, too.

I made it work this time – the card, the handshake, and all the right questions. His name was Richard and he'd just been promoted. I felt that light again, inside.

"What does your boss drive?" I asked.

He looked surprised at the question, but he told me. We had one on the lot. When I suggested he take it for a test-drive, he laughed in disbelief.

"Might as well get the practice," I said.

It got him behind the wheel. When he sat down in the deep leather seat, he looked at me and grinned. He wanted to be the man who drove this car. My heart was running. I tried not to talk too much, but it was hard. I needed this.

All through the drive, even while I recited every feature I could remember from the brochure, I was rehearsing the question in my mind. It was the big one, the tough one – eight little words that always made my mouth go dry. *Would you like to write up an offer?*

But I never had to ask.

As soon as we pulled onto the lot again, Richard got out of the car. He reached into his pocket and pulled out the business card I'd just given him.

"Listen, I'm in a hurry today. But why don't you take this into your sales manager and see what he says." He wrote a figure on the back of the card, and a phone number. "This is my cell. You can reach me any time."

I took back my card. In a glance I knew that the offer was low — really low. But it was a start. We'd negotiate up. I had a live one.

"You'll hear from me this afternoon, Richard," I said, pumping his hand. As he walked off the lot I wondered where he'd parked and what he was driving now — we hadn't talked trade-in. But it didn't matter. I could have done cartwheels back to the show-room.

"Sy wants you," Judi said as I came in.

I was still rushing, still high. I leaned my peasant's body against her work station. "Of course he does. Everybody does. You want me, don't you, Judi?" I teased.

Behind me, Dave snickered.

Judi looked at me for a second. "Try cold

water for that stain, Jens, if it's mustard."

Dave was still laughing as I walked into Sy's office, my face burning.

Sy was on the phone. He motioned at me to shut the door, which I did. But I was too excited to sit down. I paced the back of the office, reading the sales board, fingering the card with Richard's offer. I was looking at everyone's numbers but mostly Paul's. He was the one to beat, to be Sales Leader of the Month. I realized the cut-off was ten days away, the same date as my nineteenth birthday.

Behind me, Sy hung up the phone. In two strides I was at his desk, and I dropped the card on it. This close I could smell his lunch. Three shots of Glenkinchie Scotch, from Taps Bar and Grill.

"I need us to counter right away," I said. "I have to call him back."

"What the hell is this?"

I blurted out my Richard story, struggling to stay cool. But my prospect was looking at the top of our line.

"Now, I know it's low, but it's a start..."

"No, it's not, Jens. It's bullshit."

I straightened. Sy grabbed a form off his desk and thrust it at me. It was filled out, in triplicate. One of Paul's.

"This is an offer, this is real." Sy tapped my

card. "You don't even know his last name. How can I take it seriously? For all you know, this guy works for a dealer, too. He's fishing. He's trying to find out how low we'll go."

I felt struck. No wonder Richard hadn't parked where I could see, or given me one of his own business cards. But I couldn't let go.

"I'll...call him. He can come back, or I'll go to his office –"

"Jens," Sy said, getting up. "Why don't you have a chair?"

I sat down. Sy came out from behind his desk and leaned against it.

"I like you, Jens. I really do. You've got the talent and you try so hard..." He went on that this wasn't personal, it was about numbers. Who tied up a desk, how many base salaries had to be paid out. Who the producers were.

I felt waves of hot and cold breaking over me.

"I can get this guy, Sy! I think he's real. I'll get him now and write up the offer –"

I tried to stand but his hand was on my shoulder.

"One offer isn't going to solve this," Sy said gently. "Jens, I want you to take some time. Go home and relax and give yourself time to get over this."

I was really being fired. It felt like a boot in my guts.

"I can't go home," I blurted.

"Why not?"

He thought I meant to my apartment. I was talking about Ile-des-Sapins, where my family was, where my life used to be. Only one person knew what I had given up to come to Five Star Ford.

I got to my feet. "I want to talk to Mr. Lahanni."

"Jack's on holiday. And...he knows about this." A look of pain seemed to cross Sy's face. "We're all under a lot of pressure."

My head was spinning. There was nobody who could help me. I put my hand on the doorknob.

"I won't tell anybody yet," Sy said quickly. "Keep your truck for the weekend. You can bring it back Monday, when you clean out your desk."

He started over, but a look from me stopped him cold. Sy lifted his hands helplessly.

"I'm so sorry, Jens. Give yourself some time."

I nodded numbly and pushed out. That was the one thing I really didn't have.

TWO

I loved my truck, the demonstrator Jack Lahanni had arranged for me when I started. It was a white F-150XL, with a custom box that someone had ordered and never taken delivery on. When I'd gone home at Christmas, I parked in front of the house, behind Dad's glass truck, so no one in Ile-des-Sapins would miss it.

Driving back to my apartment that Friday, I parked on the street, not in my stall. I didn't want my landlord, Mr. Delbeggio, to know I was home. I owed him for half of February and all of March.

I sat down in the chair that faced the balcony, still in my suit. Late in the afternoon the sky clouded over and it began to rain. One of my windows was open, curtains flapping, water pooling on the floor, but I couldn't make myself get up to close it.

I was sure my father had never been fired. I knew he'd left school at seventeen, to help his family when his dad died. He'd had other jobs but all my life he'd been the window man. As a kid, I'd thought that was the best job you could have – fixing things that were broken, replacing old with new.

Dad worked twelve and fourteen hours a day in the summer but even when I was little, I'd wait up for him. I'd sit at the table while he ate his late dinner, happy just to look at him, big shoulders in coveralls. He'd grin across at me as if we shared a secret, and actually we did. He loved Mom but he hated parsnips, and I was the only one who saw him scrape them into the garbage.

I didn't know how to go home a failure.

A sudden banging on the door made me jump. Oh, God. Delbeggio had seen my truck. What was I going to tell him this time?

It was my brother, Daniel, dripping in the hallway. He was wearing his performance hat, an Australian cowboy hat that looked like an old-time leather fedora.

"Jens," Daniel said, "I'm in trouble, real shit this time. You've got to help me." He hesitated. "And I need twenty bucks for the cab. He's holding my guitar."

I shut the door in his face.

"Jens!" He hammered with the side of his fist, almost frantic now. "I'm not kidding. It's Mogen Kruse. He says I owe him the money — all of it! — I swear to God."

"How much is 'all of it'?" I said through the door.

When he finally spoke, I could barely hear him. "Almost five thousand dollars."

I sagged, clinging to the doorknob. I'd seen this coming, warned them about it at Christmas, but it didn't stop the blow. Five thousand dollars was a lot for any family. For ours it was a fortune.

I opened the door. "Shit for brains! Are you trying to kill Dad? Do you want him to have another heart attack?"

But I had enough money for the cab, and I gave it to him.

◆

I was the first one who believed my brother wasn't deaf. I don't remember him as a baby but I know he had a lot of ear and throat infections, that he was always on antibiotics. As a toddler he played by himself a lot. And he didn't talk. He didn't even try.

But there was something about him, a bright glimmer in his eyes as he watched me, that made me sure he was listening. At three they took him to Winnipeg for testing and got the confirmation – his hearing was fine. But still Daniel didn't talk. The adults in Ile-des-Sapins started using the word autistic, which actually sounded kind of neat because I didn't know what it meant.

The kids weren't using neat words. One afternoon a bunch of us were playing in Shane Lasko's yard and he said Daniel was a retard.

Something broke inside me. I threw myself at him, arms swinging wildly. It was my first fight and Shane was bigger than me, but I'd caught him by surprise. Once I had him down I had to keep thumping him – I was afraid he'd kill me if he got up. Mrs. Lasko dragged me off. She made my mother come and get me.

I knew what I'd done was wrong but I felt better for having answered him. You didn't say things about my family. I thought maybe someone would be proud, but my mother was just upset. She sent me to my room. When my father came home, I listened with my ear against the bedroom door. I heard the tears in my mother's voice. "I've always worried...that it might be in his blood. It's got to stop now, Karl..."

I didn't understand. Neither Shane nor I had been bleeding.

My father came in to talk to me. It was dusk and the light slanting into my room was thick gold. It lit up the dust on his work clothes. He looked tired.

"Jens," he said, "you don't hit people."

I blurted out what Shane Lasko had said and he didn't flinch. Maybe he'd already heard it.

"Daniel's not hurt," he said. "He doesn't care."

"*I* care," I said fiercely. "I thought we were supposed to stick up for our family."

"We are. Your family is the most important thing." He leaned close, and I could smell the gravel roads he'd been on. "But a strong person has self-control. You don't hit people, Jens." Dad lowered his voice. "Unless somebody hits you first."

He gave my shoulder a squeeze and I understood. This was men stuff.

We walked out to the kitchen for supper. Daniel was sitting on the floor in the living room with his Fisher-Price record player. He had a record on and he was turning it under the needle with his hand, listening to the same stretch of sound, forward, then backward, then forward again. He might have been there for hours.

"I got in trouble for you today," I whispered proudly to the back of his head. Daniel kept turning the record.

A few months later, the rumor reached our house that Mrs. Melnick wouldn't let Daniel start school if he wasn't talking. It launched something in my mom that I'd never seen, something powerful. Before she'd tended to keep Daniel at home but now she took him everywhere, tugged him along on every errand, hers and mine.

"Take your brother with you!" she'd call as I went out the door. Some days it bothered me. Who wanted a four-year-old along when you played with your friends? But secretly I was glad. I wanted him to be normal, too.

Daniel really wasn't much trouble. He was so disinterested in everyone else. He'd sit or play by himself at the edge of our game. I just had to watch that he didn't wander away.

"Keep him close," my mother warned. "I want him to hear you, listen to you, all the time."

It wasn't enough, though. At home she began to talk to him constantly, sing to him, involve him in every conversation, usually in French. I hated it. She'd never taught French to me. But it was her first language and in her panic she thought it might be his, too.

It bothered my father, who didn't speak French, either. "Jeez, Mariette, you're just going to confuse him."

My mother isn't a big woman but I saw her draw herself up in the kitchen that day. For an instant she looked larger than my dad, larger than all of us. "We don't know what he's learning right now. It can't hurt, Karl," she said quietly.

But it did hurt. It hurt me. I hated the sound of it, this language running over my head like water, too fast, too different for me to understand. It didn't matter that Daniel didn't respond. I felt utterly excluded.

"I could teach you, too, Jens," my mother said, but I didn't *want* to learn. I could talk just fine.

I decided I was going to solve this myself. I closed Daniel in our room with me.

"This is Spiderman," I said, holding up the red-and-blue toy figure for him to see. "He's got a comic, too. He's way better than Superman or Cyclops. He's the best guy. Say it. Say 'best guy.'"

Daniel looked bored. I was determined. I went through the room, my toys, which he already knew but mostly ignored.

"This is a book, Daniel. We read books. *I* can read," I said proudly, and rattled off the title. "Say 'book.'"

Nothing. He usually liked being with me but he seemed ready to leave. I dug through the closet and found something at the bottom.

"This is a xylophone. It's the only word that

starts with the letter X. You always see it up on the pictures of the alphabet. Say 'xylophone.'"

His hand was on the doorknob, trying to get out. I hit one of the keys with a pencil, just to get his attention. The high-pitched metallic note rang through the room, making him turn. I struck another key, the green one, and got a lower sound. His face lit up.

He came at me, reaching for it, but I held it away, over his head. "Say 'xylophone,' Daniel," I demanded.

I was frustrating him. He climbed onto the bed to be taller than me but I moved out of his reach. He jumped down to follow, getting angrier.

"Say 'xylophone,'" I insisted. He was making sounds in his throat as he grabbed at me, a high-pitched whine. If he cried I'd be in trouble but I wasn't giving in.

I twisted away from him. "Say it!"

"Jens!" He stamped his foot and spit out the word at the same time. I whirled around, astonished, and he grabbed the xylophone out of my hand. He dropped to the floor and began tapping on it with a piece of Lego.

"You said my name," I whispered. He ignored me now, but it didn't matter. I knew.

"Hey, I did it! I made him talk. He said my name!" I called, running out to my parents. We couldn't get anything out of him for the rest of the day, but I went to bed feeling magical. Doors opened once you knew what somebody wanted.

Language swept through Daniel that summer like a brush fire. English, French, even scraps of German — swear words my father had thought went over our heads. My mother had been right. He'd been learning all along.

He talked softly at first, and mostly to me. If a neighbor leaned over the fence and tried to engage him, it was like an assault, an invasion. He'd slip behind me and whisper, "*Scheisskopf.*" Shithead, my father's favorite curse.

But sometimes I'd hear him by himself, repeating things as if he was playing with the words.

"*Daniel, tu sais ce que c'est?* It's my mixing bowl. I'm going to make a cake."

It bothered me that he still used that language, seeing that he didn't need it. We were brothers. We were supposed to understand each other.

Then one afternoon in our room he picked up Spiderman.

"Best guy," he said.

The feeling in my chest caught me by surprise, so big I could barely hold it. No matter what, I was the one who'd started this, made him reach out of his world and into ours.

Nothing would ever change that.
"Best guy, Daniel," I said.

THREE

By the time Daniel had paid the cab driver and come back up to my apartment, I'd decided I was going to try to help him. I told myself I owed it to Mom and Dad, but underneath I was relieved to deal with some crisis other than my own. Maybe I could even fix it. Oh, God, I needed to do something right.

"Give me the guitar," I told him, opening the door just wide enough for him to pass it through. I didn't want him to see my place. I knew how bare it was.

He handed me his six-string acoustic. At home he had three more – two electric, including a pearl-front Fender Stratocaster that he'd won over the summer at SunJam, a provincial competition and concert.

I locked the apartment door behind me.

"Where are we going?" Daniel asked cautiously.

"To see Mogen Kruse," I said.

"Jens, no! He's *really* pissed at me."

"That's at you." I started down the hallway toward the stairs. "I know how to handle people."

Daniel looked surprised when we walked past the parking lot and over to the street where my truck was.

"Somebody parked in my spot," I said. I unlocked the doors. Daniel hesitated, even though he was getting wet.

"Do you want my help or not?"

He got in. I fired up the engine and pulled into traffic.

"Where's the contract? I want to see it again."

"At home. In that metal box where Mom and Dad keep all their papers locked up."

"Well, that's brilliant!"

"I didn't think I'd need it. Besides, how was I going to get it? I didn't want them to know where I was going."

"Where do they think you are?"

"I told them I was busking at the Forks," Daniel said.

"How'd you get to the city?" My brother had been sixteen for four months but he hadn't even applied for his learner's permit.

"I told them I was getting a ride."

"Yeah, you told them, but how?"

Silence.

"How?"

"Well, what do you think? I thumbed."

"Jesus, Daniel!" The fury seemed to burst in my chest and my hand swung out for him. I wanted to grab him, shake some sense into him. Instead I thumped his shoulder, maybe too hard.

"Do you want to die? Do you want some nutcase to murder you for that stupid guitar?!"

He was against the door, mad but trying to stay out of my reach. "I know, I know! Get off my case. I'm in enough shit already."

He sounded like he was on the verge of tears. I took a long breath and tried to let it go.

If we were those ice cream cones, Daniel would be Rocky Road. He's a blues guitarist, although he likes to think of himself as a performer. Personally, I don't think he sings that well. He's all right in the middle range, but his voice has a kind of raspy, frayed quality that sounds better when he's speaking the words than when he's holding a note. He says it's perfect for blues.

Daniel picked up his first guitar when he was eleven. He started to play blues when he was almost thirteen and I was fifteen. That was the year he moved out of the bedroom we shared and into the basement, by himself.

There are a lot of different kinds of blues – Chicago, Delta, Mississippi, Texas – each with its own slightly different swing and style. I don't like any of them. No matter the pace, it seems to me that blues walk. The music sounds like somebody drifting down the sidewalk with no particular place to go. I think music should run, a driving beat with a destination. I'm a rock 'n' roll man.

Daniel says that all rock, all country and almost all gospel grew out of the blues. I'm a pretty good arguer and Daniel isn't, but this is his subject and once you get him started he'll bore you to death, and take it as a win.

I never told him the truth, that what bothered me the most about blues was the hurt. They're lost-my-woman, down-on-my-luck, gonna-carve-you-up songs. Daniel was a kid. He'd lived his whole life in the same little town and he had everything. He didn't deserve to sing about pain. When he started to write those songs, it seemed like the biggest joke in the world.

Mogen Kruse didn't think so. A producer with a small recording studio in Winnipeg, he saw Daniel at SunJam and gave him his card. A lot of performers build up credibility and an audience for themselves by producing a demo cassette — a CD if they can afford it — which they sell any chance they get, at performances or even busking.

By December, Kruse had convinced Daniel and my parents that nobody gets their tape into a label — even an independent company — without an agent. He told them he'd make the demo recording free of charge, and submit it as Daniel's agent. He'd also "front" the cost of making the cassette tapes.

The first time I heard about it was at Christmas. Sitting at the kitchen table, the contract in my hand, I had an uneasy feeling. I couldn't imagine how they got Dad to go along with it. My father is Mennonite German. He gave up the religion but there are things you can't leave. Old World caution is in the blood.

"When do you have to pay Kruse back for the tapes?" I asked.

"Well, all along, as I sell them," Daniel said, fidgeting in his chair.

"You?" My brother had played in front of four thousand people at SunJam but he wouldn't ask the clerk at the Lucky Mart where the toothpaste was.

I turned to Mom. "How much is this going to cost you?"

"It's not going to cost her anything," Daniel

cut in. "I told you, I'll sell the tapes."

I wasn't even looking at him. "You know you're going to wind up paying for it, Mom."

"Jens, I don't think this is your concern," my mother said. But her hands were clasped tightly around the coffee cup in front of her. I knew the glass truck needed new brakes, and two suppliers had phoned for money in the twenty-four hours I'd been home.

"He's just pissed off because somebody thinks I'm good," Daniel muttered.

I twisted in my chair to face him. "If he thinks you're so good, why is this in here?" I found the spot and read out loud, "For the sum of two dollars, either the Agent or the Performer can terminate this contract and all monies will be rendered payable within fifteen days of that termination."

"Well, that protects me, too," Daniel said. "He'd have to pay me whatever..."

"Except he doesn't owe you — you owe him!"

"Until he signs me with a label," Daniel said stubbornly.

"Keep dreaming, Daniel," I said in disgust. "It's what you do best."

"Jens —" Mom started.

"No, he can't help it." My brother pushed away, his chair scraping. "He's an asshole through and through."

White heat burst inside me as I leapt to my feet.

"At least I'm doing something...asshole!" I shouted after him.

When I looked back, Mom was staring at me in cold disapproval. I was embarrassed. I'd promised myself that I'd make this visit as an adult.

I drifted to the kitchen counter and leaned against it. I flipped to the end of the contract, to the page with my parents' signatures.

"Did you tie Dad up to get him to sign this?" I said, trying to lighten the uncomfortable silence.

"Why don't you ask him?" my mother said evenly.

It hit me in the heart. She knew I'd barely spoken three words to Dad since I'd been home; I couldn't meet his eyes. I'd disappointed him, and it seemed worse to me than anything Daniel could dream up.

◆

The rain had slowed to a drizzle by the time we pulled up to Kruse Studios. It was an old, renovated two-story house on an artsy street with outdoor cafes.

Something occurred to me as I cut the engine.

"Did he give you the money?" I asked. "The two bucks?"

Daniel shook his head.

I felt a shot of hope. I hadn't really understood that part of the document, but if no money had changed hands, maybe the contract was still in effect.

A small bell sounded when we walked into the front office, but no one came. Down a short hallway, I noticed a red light glowing over the studio door. Kruse was recording someone. I asked Daniel how long this could take.

"All afternoon, maybe all night," he shrugged.

I didn't have all night. I waited with my hand on the doorknob. When the light went off, I pushed my way in.

The only illumination in the narrow room was over the control board that ran like a table against the wall, a scramble of knobs and levers and dials. Through a glass window, I saw the attached recording booth, its walls covered by black, bumpy foam. Three musicians were inside – two guys and a girl, with a guitar, a keyboard and saxophone.

Kruse turned abruptly in his swivel chair. He was a slight, bony man with a stomach over his belt that was surprising on his small frame. He had long, rippled gray-brown hair to his shoulders, but it was mostly gone on the top of his head.

"Hello, Mr. Kruse, how are you today?" I stuck out my hand but he didn't take it.

"Who the hell are you? How did you get in here?"

I gestured behind me, as best I could. "The door was open. Listen, I know you're busy so I'll get right to the point..."

I heard Daniel step behind me. When Kruse saw him he stood up.

"Oh, no, you don't. I'm finished with this guy," the producer said. "There's nothing to talk about."

"Five minutes!" I blurted. "If I could just have five minutes of your valuable time, I'm sure we can sort this out." I glanced through the booth window at the musicians who were staring at us curiously.

Kruse looked, too. He was turning a little pink.

"I know you want to resolve this quickly," I said in a low voice.

The producer leaned over the table and flicked on the microphone.

"I'm sorry. I have to take a few minutes. Help yourself to a coffee."

"Does this come off our bill?" one of the men said.

Kruse herded us into another room off the reception area. Probably his office, it was crowded with a desk and a daybed. Boxes and paper-work were everywhere, piled on top of the filing cabinet as well as stacked up against the wall.

"You've really done a lot with this old house," I said. "It looks so...professional."

Kruse shut the door securely and leaned against it. "Look," he started, "I don't know who you are..."

I had a card ready. "Jens Friesen. Five Star Ford." A lie now but I needed it. "I'm Daniel's brother."

"Well, he's driving me crazy," Kruse said, tossing my card on the desk. "He must phone me four times a day. I'm trying to run a business here. I don't think he realizes I did him a favor."

"He hasn't done dick," Daniel said sullenly. I shot him a look, but it was too late.

"That garbage is what I'm talking about," Kruse said. "He's on me about what *I've* done. Do you know how many tapes this kid has sold in three months? *Fifteen.* That's a hundred and fifty bucks out of five thousand. I'm the one carrying that money."

"You said you knew people," Daniel argued. "You said you could get me a contract with a label in three months — four, tops."

Kruse was getting red in the face. "That's insane! I never would have said that!"

"But you did! You said you knew people at Icon and Home Grown..."

"I do!" Kruse glanced over his shoulder at the door, and his voice dropped. "But even when you have contacts, these things take time."

"I don't think you know anybody," Daniel said.

"Why, you ungrateful little snot..." Kruse took a step toward Daniel and it startled me back to life.

"Mr. Kruse, you're absolutely right!" I moved between them, blocking his way. "Daniel will drive you crazy. He drives *me* crazy."

The producer stopped short. I think he'd forgotten I was there.

"I'm sure my parents don't know how you've been badgered," I hurried on. "They'll be very upset when they find out. Believe me, our dad will blow a fuse. I don't think you'll have this problem anymore."

Daniel looked as if I'd hit him. Kruse's shoulders dipped a bit, relaxing, but then he shifted.

"What about my money?" he said.

"I think you'll see an improvement in that area as well." I had no idea how.

"That's not good enough. I can't keep carrying this debt. I'm not...equipped."

I couldn't tell him the truth, that my parents were less equipped than he was.

"Mr. Kruse, you made Daniel a very generous offer," I said. "You must have felt he had some special quality you wanted to work with."

The producer hesitated. "He's one hot guitarist," he admitted quietly.

I tried to control the excitement in my voice. "Now, you're the one who said these things take time. It's hardly been four months. Is that an average investment a producer makes in someone they believe has genuine talent?"

Kruse shook his head ruefully.

Ask him, Jens. Ask him for more time.

"So what is the average?" I fumbled. "How long does a professional decide he's going to invest..."

"There isn't a limit," Kruse said shortly. "Each person is different. But it's not just the time, it's the money."

"I'm...I'm sure you'll see an improvement –"

"When?"

I scrambled, grasping. "Look, we're not really talking about five thousand dollars here. That's the retail value – not what the tapes cost you." I scooped one off the desk. "What are these things, a buck apiece?"

I wasn't trying to insult him. I was trying to determine how much money we were actually talking about. But everything changed.

"Are you calling me a fraud? Are you saying I'd rip this kid off?"

I tried to cut in but it was too late. The producer jabbed a finger in Daniel's direction.

"He's not worth it. I wouldn't waste my time. He's got no voice and you can teach a goddamn chimp to play the guitar..."

"Up your ass!" My brother's hands were curled into fists.

"Daniel – shut up."

"No, he can't talk to me like that."

"I'm not talking to you at all." Kruse picked up the phone. "My lawyer is. And if you're not out of here in ten seconds, it'll be the police."

"As if you had the balls, you bullshitter..." Daniel sneered.

Kruse dropped the receiver and lunged at him. The movement went through me like an electric shock. I only meant to stop him but when I grabbed Kruse I shoved him away hard – metal banged as he hit the filing cabinet. He stayed there, staring at me, frightened. I could feel the blood running through my body.

"Two weeks," I said quietly. "The contract says we have two weeks. For two dollars."

My brother dug into his pocket and hurriedly laid the money on the desk. He must have had change from the cab.

"Those are his tapes," Kruse said, tilting his

head toward a large box on the floor. He didn't take his eyes off me.

I picked it up. It had to be heavy, packed dead solid with hundreds of cassettes, but somehow I didn't feel the weight.

"Come on, Daniel," I said as I went out.

/ FOUR

I drove back to my apartment in a daze. Daniel was silent the whole way. I think he was a little afraid of me by then, not sure what I'd do next. I was scared, too. I'm not a violent person. I've only had two fights in my whole life. I couldn't get the picture out of my mind of Kruse backed up against the filing cabinet.

When I pulled into the parking lot I said, "Wait here. I'll bring your guitar."

In my apartment I started pulling clothes out of the drawers and stuffing them into two duffle bags. I didn't know what I was going to do but I could feel that this part of my life was finished. Halfway through I decided to get changed and stripped off my suit. The way it landed across the bed reminded me of a body, how it would look after they drew a chalk outline around it. I shut off the lights, fast.

Downstairs in the foyer, I stopped and unwound two keys off my ring, then dropped them into the landlord's mailbox. I felt the clunk in the pit of my stomach. Seven months ago I'd been so excited to get this apartment, my first place on my own. Delbeggio hadn't wanted to take me as a tenant because he said the young guys always snuck out in the middle of the night and stiffed him for the rent. I was insulted. I'd told him that I was different, that I had a job and I was going to be somebody he remembered.

I hurried out of the building, trying not to run.

Daniel was leaning against the truck, but when he saw all I was carrying he jogged up to meet me and took half into his arms. He looked quizzically at the duffle bags.

"I have holidays," I said. "I might go somewhere."

We loaded it all into the back. Inside the cab, Daniel turned to me.

"Jens, what are we going to do? What are we going to tell Dad?"

My stomach plummeted. He was right – I was in this, too. I'd blundered in and made it legal, forced the money to change hands. And I already had something I didn't know how to tell my father.

"We're not going to say anything yet," I told Daniel.

"He's going to find out, in two weeks for sure..."

"I know! But maybe...we can think of something. I mean, what if we came up with the money?" I hurried on. "Nobody would have to know, then."

Daniel edged across the seat. "Do you have it?"

The heat came to my face. "No."

"Well, do you have some of it?"

"No! I've...had a lot of expenses. Lately. It costs a lot to live on your own. Now, just be quiet. I have to think."

I shoulder-checked and pulled into the traffic that led to the highway I knew so well, the road to Ile-des-Sapins. Daniel didn't say another word but I could feel his hope fill up the cab, suffocating me. It can be terrible when somebody has faith in you.

◆

I am the Chocolate King of Rosetown Senior High. I am also one of only a handful of people to ever make the Rosetown Raiders football team in their junior year.

Rosetown is famous for football. For a decade it had dominated the provincial finals and two years before I got there, they'd represented

Manitoba at the national championship, which made the town even more stuck-up than it already was, even though the school buses in kids from Ile-des-Sapins, Morden, Floret and a half dozen other places.

I am not built like a receiver, a runner. I'm built like a defensive end or tackle, solid and square-shouldered, except my legs are too long – my center of gravity isn't low enough. Coach Doerksen put me in the defensive line anyway and I should have been happy to be there – the grade ten prodigy – but I wasn't. I play the game to get the ball.

I didn't tell Dad that I'd made the team, not right away. He didn't even watch sports on TV. It seemed to me his life had always been about work.

I was ten years old when he drove me past the armed forces barracks in Winnipeg, to tell me about his first job. Through the windshield I stared out at the endless rows of bright-green lawns, every square foot of it carted from the truck by my father and two other men, using wheelbarrows.

"My hands were so blistered and swollen I couldn't get them into a pair of gloves on the second day," he said softly beside me. "I cut a canvas bag into strips and wrapped them up like that." He hesitated. "Use your brain, not your back, Jens. Be something."

The first few months of grade ten I was a running fool. I knew my job and I did it, charged like a bull into the oncoming line. But every practice, every warm-up I was out to prove something, running until I thought my lungs would burst, skipping through the obstacle tires like a highland dancer. If there was an errand, I was ready. I wanted Coach Doerksen to notice me, to know my face.

"You brown nose, Friesen," Connel Tameran sneered. "You should stick your head up your own ass, just for the change."

I didn't care. We won our first four out of five games and I was early to all of them. In warm-up laps I beat myself to stay on the heels of the fastest guys. I hadn't been born a wide receiver but I was sure I could earn it. If I just kept trying and didn't give up.

At the beginning of October we started fundraising. Everybody groaned when Doerksen started pulling out cartons of chocolate-covered almonds. There were twenty-four boxes in each, at three dollars apiece.

"I expect each of you to sell at least one carton," Doerksen said. "Get your parents to take them to the office. Anybody who can't sell one carton of these things isn't really trying."

The cardboard handle dug into my fingers as I carried it home. I'd never sold anything before but I wanted to be the first one to put that money in Doerksen's hand.

"Use your brain, Jens," I told myself.

I started in Morris, because nobody in that town was on the team — no competition. And I learned fast that even if you were nervous, you could smile at people, and they'd smile back. My little speech got better every time, but I listened to people, too. When a man told me his son had played for the Raiders the year they went to the championship, I asked for his name. At each house after that, I introduced the Raiders as "the team Gary Frechette used to play for."

It was magic. By the time I was halfway down the second side of the first street, my carton was empty and the money was a thick, doubled-over wad. I walked out to the highway again, the prairie night clean and crisp and studded with stars.

This is something, I told the sky.

The next day I turned in the money — the first one — and I took two more cartons. I sold between two and three cartons a night, every night after that, in towns that reached to the edge of Winnipeg. When the blitz was over, I'd sold fifty-one cartons — 1,224 boxes of chocolate-covered almonds at three dollars each. And when Connel Tameran blew out the ligaments in his knee near the end of the season, Ronnie Lews got bumped up to running back and Jens Friesen became a wide receiver for the Rosetown Raiders. I didn't score a single touchdown but I was happy to get the ball.

I finally told Dad that I was playing, and he came out to watch me when he could. Some parents are screamers, but my father never said a word. He wouldn't even sit down. He stood in the aisle with his hands in his pockets, and on the drive home he'd let me talk. Yet the sight of him up in the stands was all the cheering I needed.

In grade eleven, I was a receiver from day one. But I never slacked off. I went into every practice, every game as if I was still trying to win my position. It made a difference. I was more agile than the goons coming at me and I could run like the north wind. Rosetown became known as a passing team, and a lot of the time they were passing to me.

In that October's fundraising blitz I sold eighty-nine cartons of chocolate-covered almonds. And that's when I met Jack Lahanni.

It was right after a practice. I was trooping into the school to shower, the heat and smell of that hour beaming off me like radiation, and I heard, "That's him. That's the one. Jens!"

I turned. Coach Doerksen is over six feet tall,

but he seemed dwarfed by the man who stood beside him. I knew who it was. I almost stumbled as I walked up.

"Jens, this is Jack Lahanni. I was telling him about you," Doerksen said.

My head was spinning. Was I being scouted?

The big man thrust out his hand and shook mine, the Grey Cup ring like a brilliant golf ball. My finger brushed it in the grip.

"I hear you're quite a salesman," Jack Lahanni said.

"I try," I said, my mind still trying to take in that he was here, that he was speaking to me.

"He holds the record," Doerksen said quickly. "I've never seen anything like it. He's sold more of those damn chocolates than anyone in the history of the school, maybe the province. But he's like that. Keeps going and..."

"I saw that," Jack Lahanni said, smiling at me. "If you died on that field you wouldn't have the sense to lie down."

"No, sir, I wouldn't — I promise," I blurted.

Jack Lahanni laughed, a deep, encouraging rumble. He turned toward the school parking lot and began to amble slowly. I was already taller than my father but I still couldn't match his stride.

We didn't talk about football. He asked me what I was going to do once I finished school. I was a math and science major, making decent marks, but I really didn't know. Dad had been talking about university but that didn't seem...big enough. I wanted to be something.

"So, tell me, Jens," Jack said finally. "The day's done at 3:30, your friends go home and you're out there running your ass off for another hour. Why? What's so important?"

The only thing that came to my mind was the truth.

"I want the ball," I said. "Every time, every play. I can't help it. All I want is to get the ball."

Jack stopped abruptly, his eyes glittering like the huge ring on his hand.

"That," he said, "is drive. And I don't know why some people have it and others don't. You can teach people just about anything, but you can't make them want something. Believe me, I've tried."

He nodded toward the field.

"Drive is the most important thing you take out there, Jens. And you know what? It works in other places, too. Pointed in the right direction, it could make you a lot of money." For the first time I saw the silver car in the parking lot, glinting chrome and steel. Drive had made Jack Lahanni a lot of money.

He reached into his pocket and pulled out a business card. I took it with two hands, like a gift.

"When you're ready, you call me," he said.

The gold-embossed letters seemed gilded onto the paper. *Five Star Ford, New cars and trucks, Jack Lahanni, Proprietor.*

It was time to shake his hand goodbye but I was lost in a daze, still holding the card. Instead he gave me a solid, friendly thump on the back.

"When you're ready," he said again, starting toward his car.

I woke up.

"I will!" I called. "Thank you, Mr. Lahanni! I won't forget. Thank you!"

He waved as he swung in behind the wheel. I put the card in my wallet, in one of the plastic sleeves to protect it.

That spring Dad had the heart attack. The fancy name for it is coronary thrombosis. It means a clot has cut off the blood supply to an area of the heart, which damages it. But if the damaged area is small and doesn't impair heart-beat, the attack shouldn't be fatal. I know this because I read every paragraph on it in our Family Medical Guide, over and over.

Daniel and I were allowed to see him two days later. He was in the coronary-care unit of the Health Sciences Centre in Winnipeg, and he'd already had surgery that opened the blocked section of his artery.

Mom took us in, one hand on each of our

shoulders. I felt a kick, like a foot in my stomach. I don't think I'd ever seen my father in bed — we weren't even allowed into our parents' bedroom and he was always up before us, anyway. He'd never had a cold so bad it kept him home. Now he was lying there, one tube in his nose, another in his arm, a machine still monitoring his heartbeat. I looked away, as if I'd just caught him naked. This was the man who used to hold out his arm to let me swing on it.

When he came home, everything changed. How we ate, what we did, who we saw. Everybody in town seemed to come by — once. I felt people looking at me, the oldest, the biggest son.

My mother went to work at the Capital Cafe, in Ile-des-Sapins' only hotel. She'd never been a waitress before but she made more in tips than she did for a salary. She's a pretty woman. With her dark hair tied back and the dusty rose uniform outlining her trim body, she was more than pretty. The women in Ile-des-Sapins said Mariette did so well because people felt sorry for my dad. The men didn't say anything. I couldn't bring myself to go into the Capital Cafe, not even for a Coke, once she started there.

My eighteenth birthday came and went. That summer I worked four afternoons a week at the

Rosetown Food Fare, unloading boxes from the big trailers, and it didn't feel like enough. I spent a lot of time firing a lacrosse ball at the old wooden shed in our back yard. I never broke through but I cracked it in a lot of places.

Dad was home the whole summer. He was encouraged to walk but not a whole lot more than that. All day he paced in the house or played solitaire at the kitchen table. I'll always remember the summer by that sound, the frustrated *snap, snap* of cards against wood. I could hear it no matter where I was in the house, even above the sound of Daniel's guitar drifting up from the basement. My father didn't cheat. I never saw him win.

In the fall I started grade twelve, and Dad cautiously began to feel out the small jobs. But there was such a backlog of bills that we all still tensed when the phone rang. And most days I would come home from school and see him at the kitchen table, his broad shoulders twitching as he snapped down the cards of that stupid game.

That's when I was ready. I put on my sport-coat and got a ride to the city with Mr. Gregoire, who took me all the way in to Five Star Ford. Jack Lahanni was surprised to see me — he knew I wasn't supposed to graduate until the next June — but when I explained the circumstances he was good to his word. I came home flushed with the package he'd promised me: the training, base-plus-commission, even a demonstrator to drive.

"Jens," my father said, angry beyond shouting, his hand gripping my arm at the kitchen table. "Don't do this, for God's sake. This isn't the life you want. If you leave school now, you might never get back."

"And maybe I don't want to," I argued. "Look, it's time for me to do this, contribute something..."

"It's my job to support us, not yours."

"I'm not talking about that," I lied, pulling out of his grip. "Listen, I'm good at sales. I've got drive. I can make money, real money..."

"This isn't about money, is it?" Dad's voice was hushed. "Jens, what do I have to say to you? You don't have to prove anything to me. You don't have to earn your place in this family."

He was too close. I stood up, heart pounding.

"You don't understand anything! I want *my* life, not the one you didn't have. And the world's different now. Success happens for people who go out and get it."

He straightened in his chair. "I think I know how the world works."

"What do you know, Dad? You know windows."

It was too far and I knew it. My father stood up. He walked out of the kitchen.

"This is going to work," I called after him. "You'll see! You're going to be so..."

He was gone. I was sick, scalding with shame. In the darkened hallway beyond the kitchen I saw the faint glimmer of a face, then the figure that hung back in the shadow, listening.

"Get the hell away from me," I whispered to my brother. "If I see your face I'll break it."

/FIVE

It was full darkness when I pulled the truck into the driveway behind my parents' house, beside the ramshackle shed my father said was an old garage but was too small to even hold a car. The kitchen windows beamed out at me, yellow and warm against the black yard. I'd never meant to come home like this — come home because I had to.

Daniel opened his door and I came to life. "Let me do the talking," I said. "You can't lie worth shit. Leave the tapes in the truck until I think of something."

We got his guitar out of the back but before I closed the hatch, he stopped me.

"Jens, give me some money. Just a few bucks. I always show her what I earned."

"Big man," I snorted, pulling out ten dollars,

the last money in my pocket. "I want it back," I said.

I made him go first, ahead of me. My mother must have heard the truck because she flung the door open as soon as we stepped onto the walk.

"What's the matter? What happened? Your dad went to look for you."

"All the way to the Forks?" Daniel was horrified. Dad had driven an hour and a half each way to check a place he hadn't been.

"Well, that's what you told me," she snapped. "I didn't know where else you would go."

"He came to see me," I said.

"Jens..." Mom seemed to notice me in the darkness for the first time. "Why?"

"No big deal, he just did," I said, but I turned my face away as I trooped past her. I didn't know if I was a better liar than Daniel.

The kitchen smelled like dinner and I inhaled a deep breath. I could tell it was rouladen in the oven, a thin cut of beef rolled up with onions and bacon that you roasted the hell out of and drowned in gravy. My mouth was watering. It had been a long time.

My mother looked from Daniel to me as she closed the door, her radar at work. Walking past Daniel she leaned in close, head tilted. It was an odd movement, as if she was...smelling him.

Daniel whipped out the ten dollars and waved it proudly in front of her.

"I got it changed. There was more but I spent some."

She plucked the money out of his hand. "Good. Now you only owe me twelve."

Daniel was surprised but not more than me. That was my money!

"La musique. Tu te souviens pas? Est-ce que t'as pas dit, Mom, je te paierai après?"

Daniel wilted, she must have had him dead to rights. But their private language was a slap. They wouldn't do it in front of Dad. I took an angry step toward the door.

"Well, I got him home," I said.

Mom threw her arms around my shoulders, a hug that held me back.

"Jens, I'm so glad to see you. Can you stay for supper?"

My mom tries, I know she does. But Daniel was a baby with ear infections. He was a toddler who didn't speak. I'm always her second thought, I know that. I've forgiven her.

"Of course he can stay," Daniel said, shrugging off his jacket. "He's on holidays."

I gave him a sharp look. I was supposed to do the talking.

"Already? You haven't been there a year," Mom said.

There was the crunch of gravel, and a sound I'd have known in my sleep – the squeak of my father's brakes. My stomach pulled into a tight ball.

"There he is." Mom let me go. "I'll tell him Daniel's home. He was so worried." She went into the living room to the front door. I stepped in front of my brother, backing him against the counter.

"Just shut up. Don't say anything about me, or you're in this on your own, I swear."

Daniel's eyes widened. He didn't know what he'd done wrong. I heard my name in the conversation and turned.

My father was in his work clothes, padded overalls of gunmetal blue. The color looked too bright next to his face, creased by lines I couldn't remember seeing at Christmas. His hair seemed paler, not turning silver or gray but just fading. The heart attack had been over a year ago but somehow the last few months had compressed him, flattened him. It worried me.

Dad put his hand on Daniel's head as if to ruffle his hair, but instead he pushed, short and sharp. He was mad.

Daniel staggered back a step, shaken.

"*Scheisskopf!* Your mother was worried sick."

"I'm sorry! I went to see Jens," Daniel blurted.

"So? He doesn't have a phone?"

Actually, I didn't. It had been disconnected two weeks ago.

"We got talking," I said quickly. "He just forgot."

Dad looked at me for the first time, and almost smiled. "Hello, stranger," he said. His hand moved, as if to reach for me, but instead he gestured at my clothes.

"You wearing that jacket to the table?"

We got down to business. In the Friesen house, meals are business. We're not bean sprout people, no fancy sauces looped on the plates.

"I just lay it out and stand back," my mom likes to say, and that's exactly what she did. Daniel's never had much of an appetite and when he's upset, he loses it completely. Nothing slows me down. I love food. Thank God I've always had the metabolism and the frame for it, that peasant's body. I was so hungry and the spread of it, the smell of home that rose up from dish after dish, was like a hug.

"It's good to see somebody eat around here," my father said, plunking the gravy down next to me, something he wasn't allowed to have anymore. I knew it cheered him up just to watch me. "How's work?"

My heart was in my throat.

"Good," I managed.

"Think you might have some time?"

"Jens is on holidays right now," Mom cut in.

"Holidays," my father repeated. It was a foreign concept in our house.

"It...it's so busy in the summer. Everybody wants a new car because they're going out on the highway. And then the new models come out in the fall. They told us to take our holidays now." I felt pinned by his clear blue eyes. "Why? What do you need, Dad?"

"I thought maybe we'd tear down that shack of an outhouse and build a real garage," Dad said.

"Karl! You are not hauling lumber, you are not laying cement..."

My father waved her objections away. "I'm not going to lift a finger, except maybe to point. This One and That One, they'll do the heavy work."

The words were like a warm hand on my shoulder. He used to call us that when we were kids, pet names full of pride. This One and That One. I had always been This One.

Daniel looked faintly sick — the guitar man hated heavy work. But I suddenly knew I didn't need him. I could build this thing by myself if Dad just told me what to do. He'd been talking about that garage for years and I wanted to finally make it happen.

Something occurred to me.

"How much is it going to cost?"

"Between four and five thousand," Dad said through a mouthful.

"Do you have it?" I said without thinking.

He smiled and kept chewing. In the Friesen household, kids didn't ask adults what they could afford. He surprised me when he spoke again.

"I will soon. That seniors' complex that's going up in St. Andrew's? I got the contract. It's a big bejesus job but I think I can swing it."

"You should hire someone to help you," my mother said. "Get Don Shibote."

Dad didn't seem to hear. He was talking to me, his eyes lit up. "If all I have to pay for is materials, and we do the work on weekends, we could get the walls and roof up before I get busy in the summer. Hell, we might even get it insulated."

"Dad, that's great!" I said, and I meant it. After what we'd gone through in the last year, this moment seemed like a miracle.

Except he'd have to give the money to Mogen Kruse.

I looked at Daniel. His eyes were fixed on his plate, avoiding me. He'd known about this. He'd known it when he'd thumbed into the city to aggravate the hell out of Kruse.

In that instant I almost hated him, the self-centered little prick. He pushed and pushed for what he wanted, and he didn't care who had to pay for it.

"How's school, Daniel?" I said evenly.

He looked up. "It's...okay."

My father pushed his plate away. "That's right. Report cards." He held his hand out, all business. "Where is it?"

My mother leapt to her feet. "Oh, you can see it after, Karl. Let's have dessert."

She set out another one of my favorites, a coffee slice with caramel icing. My father bit into his low-fat cookie, resigned.

Daniel was glaring at me.

"You know, they're already selling tickets to your grad, to the ceremony," my brother said. "I heard Chris Butler had to buy six because his whole family is going. His grandma is going to fly in from Vancouver, it's such a big deal."

Beside me, my father's breath ran out in a sigh, as if someone had thrust a knife into a tire.

I went to my room after dinner. My old room. I remembered how it had been when Daniel and I both slept there, the beds against connecting walls, ends almost touching. I remembered us sitting up on our elbows, whispering in the dark, in the days when I was the only one he would talk to. Even after he could talk, he didn't much, except at night. Then his whole day seemed to pour out of him, like he was a full glass that finally overflowed.

My brother had never done really well in school. He was smart but he just wasn't interested; he daydreamed a lot. Because he was so quiet, the rumor persisted that he was at least partially deaf, and maybe half retarded. Sometimes kids called him things just to see if he'd react. But if I was there, they kept their mouths shut. I tried to be there.

Then, at the end of my grade nine year, I got into the second fight of my life, with Chris Butler. It wasn't about Daniel, but it changed everything. My brother moved into the basement with his guitars. Late at night he'd still be playing, his noise vibrating the floor under my feet. I'd yell down the heating vent at him, tell him to shut the hell up.

Now my room was exactly as I'd left it — school binders dumped on the desk, sports bag open against the wall, lacrosse stick leaning against the dresser that was piled with books. I pawed through the clutter as if I could find the money hidden somewhere.

If only we could sell the tapes. But how? Who would buy them? Busking didn't work. Fifteen tapes in three months, Kruse had said. But that was Daniel, not the Chocolate King.

I hesitated, my hands on a drawer, an idea flickering.

Dad's voice rumbled through the wall, the rising pitch of anger. Shit! Daniel must have told him. I pushed off the dresser and hurried to the kitchen.

My father's fading hair had tumbled over his forehead, shaken out by the force of his stride, up and down the room. He had papers in his hand. Oh, God — the contract. I froze in the doorway.

Daniel was slumped in a chair at the table, staring at his locked fingers. Mom was behind him, lips pursed as she tried to watch them both at the same time, a referee or guardian or both. But I knew she wouldn't interfere.

"Do you think I'm a fool, is that it? Do you think you can make a deal — a promise — and then ignore it? I'm such a fool I'm going to forget?"

Daniel shook his head, a bare quiver.

"Talk, dammit! I want you to talk to me."

"No!" It took effort for him to get the word out.

"No, what?"

"No, I don't think you're a fool."

"Then why would you do this? Let it go on and on and not even try?"

Daniel looked up for the first time, his eyes a dark blaze. "I did try."

"Bullshit. Trying is studying. Trying is getting help – asking for help. It's not sitting in the basement playing the goddamn guitar. Well, they're in lock-up now, mister..."

"You can't –"

"Not only that," Dad continued, "I am phoning this Kruse guy tomorrow and I'm telling him it's off. Whatever he's doing, he's going to stop right now..."

"Dad!" My voice rang across the room and all three turned to look at me. My father straightened, pulled up the waistband of his pants. He gestured at me.

"This is your doing," he said.

The words were a blow.

"What? How?"

He thrust the sheets out at me. I strode over and caught them up. It wasn't the contract, it was Daniel's second term report card. Fragments of sentences leapt out at me: "...assignments incomplete...does not attend regularly..." I read them in disbelief. He was failing.

"This is your example," Dad said. "He looks to you. When you gave up, he gave up."

The heat was in my face, the fire I'd been avoiding – we'd both been avoiding – for seven months.

"I didn't give up. I withdrew."

"You quit," he seemed to spit out the words,

"when you could have done it, finished no problem, sailed through one last year. You're smart, Jens. You could have graduated and been something."

"I am something!"

"And what is that? Someone with a shiny car? Possessions...aren't a life. Even thieves can have shiny new cars."

"This isn't about me." I was scrambling, trying to deflect those piercing eyes away from me. "Daniel is responsible for his own life, his own grades." I tossed the pages onto the table. "This isn't my fault."

My father seemed to sag, condense just a little more. "No, it's mine. I couldn't stop you, and you won't stop him. But we had a bargain, and I keep my promises."

He began to walk away.

"Karl..." Mom's voice was a shock in the room. It ignited me.

"Don't call Kruse," I blurted.

Dad stopped but didn't turn around.

"Daniel can still improve," I said. "There's a semester left."

"I am done talking to That One."

"So let me talk to him! Give me a week. I've got a week. We'll...go camping."

My brother tried to cut in – the guitar man hated camping, too – but I rolled right over him.

"Maybe you're right. Maybe it's my fault. So just let me try this," I pleaded to my father's back. "You don't have anything to lose. He's off school, anyway. Please, Dad."

My father turned at last, weary but not beaten. I could see in his face that he thought the whole conversation was pointless.

"I think they should do it," Mom said. "Go and look after themselves for awhile. If you want them to learn responsibility, that's a good way." Her quiet voice seemed to take over the kitchen. "It couldn't hurt, Karl."

Later, in my room, I rifled my drawers for extra clothes to take. Daniel was on my bed, leaning back on his elbows, knees up so I could hardly see him. I was telling him how it would work.

"We'll sleep in the tent – you know that two-man job we used to put up in the back yard? We'll go to campgrounds, or just wherever we can pull over and park. Rest stops. Then we'll drive into the little towns. I mean *little* – places where they're starved for entertainment. If they have a bar, or a restaurant, I'll get you in there. You'll work for nothing if you have to, but we'll sell those tapes."

"So when are you going to fix me, Jens?" he said, his voice icy. "When are you going to make me better, make me smart?"

I slammed the drawer shut. "You're going to fix yourself. You're going to get your act together and stop this crap." I stood up and turned on him. "You're not fooling anybody, Daniel. You're not dumb. I don't know how you could do this to him..."

He seemed to leap off the bed. "Do what? What did I do to him?!"

"You lied. You said you'd pick up your grades so he'd sign the contract. You never intended to follow through."

"That's not true!"

"It is! I know you. You don't care if you break his heart. Everything's for you." My voice dropped. "And on top of that, you go and bug the hell out of Kruse, the man who's doing you a favor, pester him to death because the only person who has a life is you."

Daniel's hands were clenched. I could see the tendons standing out on his arms. "Yeah, I wanted to know how things were going, what he was doing. Why not? The guy's going to make money off me."

"Oh, right. And you were a real star in there today."

"And what the hell were *you*?"

A welt of heat was burning me. This close I realized he was taller than I remembered, even than he'd been at Christmas.

"Get some money from Mom," I said finally. "As much as she can spare. She'll give it to you — anything for her baby."

He didn't slam the door, not quite.

SIX

I'd slept in that bed for most of my life and I loved it, but I woke up with a sick feeling. I'd forgotten something important. Daniel and I needed transportation, but the truck was supposed to go back Monday. I had to beg Sy for a few more days.

I had a quick shower and crept out of the house to the pay phone beside the Lucky Mart.

When Judi answered, I lowered my voice to disguise it and asked for Sy.

"I'm afraid he's no longer with us," Judi said. "Can someone else help you?"

I was stunned. I'd only been gone one afternoon. Had Sy quit or been fired?

"What happened to Sy?" I said, forgetting myself.

There was a pause. "Who is this?" Judi demanded. "Do I know you?"

I panicked and hung up.

I stood in the chilly morning, my hand still on the phone, my breath puffs of vapor hanging in the air. Jack was on vacation and now Sy was gone, too. Did anyone know about me? I needed this truck.

Even thieves can have shiny new cars.

But I wasn't stealing, I was just borrowing. I only needed it for a few days — a week, tops. Whatever had happened to Sy, the dealership would be in some chaos. Maybe no one would notice me missing right away. I could always call in Monday and talk to the accountant, Henry. If he asked, I'd tell him Sy told me to keep it a week.

And that was lying.

But not today. I hadn't done it yet, didn't know that I would. Right now I needed the truck and I had it. I was still okay.

I went into the store, to the bank machine at the back, and withdrew the last fifty dollars out of my account. Then I walked home softly, as if the ground was eggshells.

I went downstairs to the basement that had become Daniel's room. It was still the laundry room, but he'd piled plastic soft-drink crates in a wall that sectioned his bed off in one corner.

His life was scattered everywhere – stacks of CDs, a large amp and a smaller one, magazines, song sheets and his guitars: the acoustic, the Mann electric, the Fender Stratocaster and a mandolin-shaped thing I didn't know the name of.

Taped to the cement wall by his bed was a big, brilliant poster of Colin James. Technically James isn't a bluesman – he's a blistering rock 'n' roll guitarist. But he came from small-town Saskatchewan and he started playing in blues clubs when he was thirteen.

I don't know much about music but I know there are a lot of old blues masters: brothers Stevie Ray and Jimmie Vaughn, B.B. King – hell, even Hendrix and Clapton. I don't know why my brother chose the hero he did.

Daniel had just woken up. He was sitting on the edge of his bed in his underwear and a T-shirt, his long legs bare. I could see his shoulder blades, sharp angles poking up through the fabric, and I felt a pang. God, he was thin.

I dropped to one knee on the carpet beside his bed, like a coach in the huddle.

"Okay," I said quietly, "get dressed and pack – warm things and then something to perform in, not your usual grubby stuff. I'll get the sleeping bags and everything else. I'll leave the truck open and I want you to sneak some guitars in."

I glanced at their black cases against the wall. "Take the acoustic and both electrics." I wanted a back-up in case something broke. "And an amp, and cords, and whatever else you need. Don't let Mom and Dad see you do it. Did you get some money?"

"Not...yet."

I felt an impatient pulse. This was critical. "Well, do it." I started toward the stairs. "Now hurry up. We'll have a big breakfast before we go."

"I'm not hungry," he muttered behind me.

I whirled around. "Yes, you are!"

He stared at me from under the dark, messy tumble of his hair, surprised.

"You've got to eat, Daniel," I said, shrugging. "Build yourself up."

I jogged up the stairs into the smell of frying bacon. Mom was at the counter, cracking eggs into a blue bowl she'd always used to mix pancakes. Her dark shoulder-length hair was pulled back in a ponytail. It amazed me, sometimes, that I could look down on the top of her head, that women in general are so little. From behind you'd think she was a Rosetown girl.

I was suddenly next to her, looking for something to steal – bacon or a piece of toast. She elbowed me away.

"Sit down. I want to serve it all at once," she

said, but smiling. "I aired out the sleeping bags last night." She grated fresh cinnamon into the batter. "They're on the line outside."

"Thanks."

"The tent and the propane hotplate – I think they're both in the shed. Don't forget toilet paper, and soap and shampoo." She glanced over her shoulder at me. "Where are you going to wash?"

I didn't answer because I hadn't even thought of it. But she knew that.

"Some of the campgrounds have showers, but most of them have sinks, anyway. The ones that are open. You can always stop at gas stations. Where are you going to go?"

"I don't know. Just around. Hey, it's an adventure," I said lightly.

She turned, grinning at me. "If you forget the toilet paper, *then* it's an adventure." Her smile tightened. "I'm going to worry. I'm telling you that now. I want you to phone every day."

Yet she had agreed with my plan, argued for it last night. She was on my side and I didn't know why.

She turned back to the griddle, lifting the edges of the pancakes to check underneath, although it was too soon.

"Take some canned food from the pantry and I'll set out pots and pans you can use. I don't want you taking my good pots. And, Jens...don't let him drink."

"Drink what?"

"You know. Liquor. Beer. Anything."

"Daniel doesn't drink," I said. But in my mind's eye I saw it again, that strange moment when she'd leaned forward to smell him. I remembered the shock of that report card in my hand. Daniel was sixteen. He was going to Rosetown Senior High. I knew that town, all the houses you could go to, all the people who would take you in.

I straightened in my chair. "What the hell is he up to? Does Dad know about this?"

She looked at me, a warning glance to calm me down.

"I don't know for sure, Jens. I just *think*. So don't go..."

The door to the basement opened, stopping us. Daniel looked from one to the other.

"Go where?" he said.

"Just...go," I said smoothly. "I've got a map. I'm figuring out our route."

"I want to go through Easton," Daniel said, dropping into a chair across from me.

"Easton! Why?"

"I just do, okay? I know somebody who lives there."

I had no idea how he could have met somebody from that far away. The town was four hours past Winnipeg, and not the direction I had planned. I wanted to drive toward Ontario, because there were more towns closer together. No way were we going to waste time in Easton.

"We'll see," I said.

The pancakes weren't ready but Mom laid out the rest of it, a plate piled with crisp bacon, toast, juice, fruit sliced into little bowls – the full treatment. I dove into it, not bothering with silverware. At home, almost everything can be finger food.

It bothered me about Daniel, how he might have been wasting his afternoons. It was a slap in the face to Mom and Dad and...it bothered me. He didn't have anything to drink about.

I looked across the table. He was swirling his orange juice, playing with it.

"How's Keith Klassen doing? Did he make the Raiders?" I said.

Keith was in my brother's year, but he was big and tough enough to play pick-up games with the older guys in Ile-des-Sapins.

"How should I know?" Daniel said.

"I bet he has his own fan club," I continued. "Rosetown girls really go for the buff guys. He'll have to peel them off."

My mother shot me a glance, but I pretended not to see it.

"I mean, that's how it works. You don't even

have to make the team, just look like it. Give them something to hang onto, and they will," I said, grinning. Daniel rolled his eyes but he picked up his cutlery and started to poke around, finally. I went to the fridge and poured us each a tall glass of milk. When I set one in front of my brother, I let go a short sigh.

"Daniel, you don't cut up fruit."

"I like it in smaller pieces."

"It's in a bowl. You don't cut anything that's in a bowl."

"You're an expert at that, too? You do women and fruit?"

I was suddenly angry. "At least I know what's normal. You're afraid to get dirty. That's sick. It's delusions of greatness or something."

"So I'm not a savage! I don't have to dive in there and squeeze it to death..."

I leaned back in my chair, threw up my arms. "I'm a guitarist, don't touch me, don't touch my hands!"

The solid thunk of a plate on the table jolted me upright.

"You're going camping, the two of you?" Mom said. "In a tent, together?"

Daniel and I glanced at each other, embarrassed. "Yeah," I said.

"I wish I could sell tickets," Mom said.

After breakfast I went outside to pack up the

truck. I was starting to get scared. What if this didn't work? What was I going to do about the truck on Monday? And I'd been fired. What kind of salesman could I be if Jack and Sy didn't believe in me anymore?

The tent, stove and propane tank were sitting on the grass next to the shed. Dad had dug them out and cleaned them up; the metal parts shone in the sun. I'd been avoiding him since last night, his words still in me like whiplash: This is your doing.

And yet here were these things I needed laid out like a gift. I dropped to one knee, pretending to check over the stove, but the knobs glittered at me through water.

I can do this, I promised. I can make it right. And I'll come back and build that garage, all by myself.

After I loaded the gear, Daniel and I managed to sneak the guitars in. Mom and Dad both came out to see us off. We all stood awkwardly in the sunshine, stalling. Mom gave a last-minute speech − instructions, good advice. My father stood silently with his hands in his pockets. I'd figured out long ago that my parents took care of different family departments: Mom was Health and Safety; Dad was Character.

Finally Mom threw her arms around me in a hug.

"Don't lose him, Jens," she whispered.

Dad pulled Daniel in around the shoulders, buffed the top of his head with an Old World kiss. "Listen to your brother," he said.

He didn't say anything to me. When I reached out to shake his hand he clasped it with both of his, hard. I was suddenly blinking, my throat tight. I couldn't say goodbye, either.

We were already in the truck when Daniel looked alarmed.

"Wait a minute," he said, and darted into the house. He came out with something in his hand — that damned fedora!

My insides sank. Oh, yeah, just advertise it, Daniel.

"Why do you need the hat?" Mom said.

Daniel climbed into the cab and hung out the window. "I don't know — luck?"

I started the engine and swung out backwards, a fast arc that swept us into the street. We all waved, smiling, but in my rearview mirror I caught a glimpse of them as I drove away: Character and Health and Safety standing shoulder to shoulder with the same taut face.

SEVEN

I could have driven through Ile-des-Sapins with my eyes closed and not missed a turn. But I took my time, pausing at every stop sign, even the ones that didn't count. Daniel was sitting forward on the edge of his seat, as if we were on our way to the Red River Ex.

"Put your seatbelt on," I said. "Did you get the money?"

He gave me an irritated glance but clicked it dutifully in place.

"Yeah, I did."

I held out my hand. "Give it to me."

"Why should you always hold the money?"

It was true. Let loose at the fair or even sent to the corner store, I was always the one given the money, for both of us. It was logical – I was older, more responsible. Plus I thought it was one of the privileges of being born first.

"Because I won't lose it," I said.

He struggled to reach past the seat belt and into his pocket. "I've never lost anything, not even a guitar pick," he grumbled, but he handed it over.

I felt the single bill in my hand, then looked at it to be sure.

"This is it?! Twenty bucks?"

"That's all she would give me," he sputtered. "She says, 'What do you need money for?'"

We had reached the edge of town, the stop sign where main street met the highway. I hesitated, the engine running.

"We don't have enough," I said. "Between this and what I have, it's not enough for even two tanks of gas."

"Well, don't you have more...somewhere?" Daniel said hopefully.

"No! I told you, I've had expenses. You don't know what it costs to live on your own."

His mouth twisted. "That's my brother. Big truck, no gas."

I could have shaken him, this kid who'd never had to pay his own way. But I had another plan, a loose idea I'd been saving for later, in case we were desperate. Later was suddenly now and Daniel wasn't going to like it.

I put on my turn signal and pulled onto the highway that led to Winnipeg.

"Where are we going?" he said.

"To the city." I took a breath. "We're going to pawn the Fender."

"Bull shit we are!"

"We're not selling, we're pawning. We'll get it back," I argued.

"Bull shit! That's my guitar. Mine. I won it. I'll never get another one, not like that." He was wild. I was glad he was belted in.

"Daniel, listen to me..."

"No, Jens. No way!"

I swerved onto the side of the road and hit the brakes, spraying gravel.

"Okay. Then I'll turn around right now and you'll march in and say, 'Dad, I screwed up. I screwed up *again*. I need five thousand bucks. Sorry about your garage.'"

The words stopped him, shook the wild energy out of him. Now he just glared at me.

My heart was pounding. I was more afraid to go home than he was. "Those are your choices," I said.

Finally he looked away. "That's my guitar," he said to the window.

I eased the truck into gear, relieved.

"We'll get it back. I promise."

He didn't say another word, but sat clutching

the fedora, curling up the battered brim all the way to Winnipeg.

I knew where I was going. I'd driven past the place enough times, a few blocks off the city's main street. Mickey's was probably the biggest pawn shop in Winnipeg; the sign painted on the side of the building said they even took cars and snowmobiles. Still, it was on a street that had been fading for fifty years, across from the Salvation Army Thrift Store and a place that cashed cheques.

I parked in the back. I didn't wait for Daniel but opened the hatch and found the right case. I was on the sidewalk in front of the building when he appeared beside me.

Through the first door and up the stairs, we were stopped by metal bars. I rattled them.

"Just a minute," a woman's voice cried out. There was a harsh buzzing and I pushed through the security gate.

The place was big, a two-story warehouse packed full, and I knew I wasn't seeing all of it. Against one wall were washers and dryers, TVs and VCRs. On the floor were revolving racks of video cassettes and CDs, and there was a huge glass counter of gold and diamond rings. They were set carefully into displays but didn't glitter, somehow. The first shine had already rubbed off.

I didn't see any musical instruments, but I knew there was a second floor.

A woman of about forty was sitting behind the counter, her generous hips balanced on a small stool, brassy red hair to her shoulders.

"Can I help you guys?"

Daniel hung behind me like a shadow.

I stuck out my free hand to shake hers. "Hi! How are you today?"

She looked amused. "Pretty good. What about you?"

"I've been better. Nobody comes here when things are great, right?"

She eyed the case I was holding. "That's the song. What do you have to show me?"

"Something to make your day," I said, setting it on the counter. I opened the case with a flourish and lifted it up by the neck, trying to get the overhead light to flash on the pearl front plate. "That's a Fender Stratocaster."

"I can read," she said, her eyes running appraisingly over the guitar. "Is it yours?"

"It's mine. I won it," Daniel said. He'd already drifted away to the rack of CDs, as if he didn't want to stand close to us.

She glanced from me to him. "Are either of you boys eighteen?"

"Me," I said.

"Got I.D.?"

"Driver's license," I said, reaching for my wallet.

"Then it's his guitar," she told Daniel. His face seemed to tighten.

"How much do you want?" she said to me.

I leaned my Rosetown Raiders' body against the counter toward her and grinned.

"A million bucks?"

She grinned back. "A hundred and fifty."

"I was hoping for more..." I said with my best disappointed sigh. She glanced over the guitar again.

"Two hundred, but that's the top. I've got a lot of guitars."

"Okay," I said.

"Are you nuts?!" Daniel flew out from behind the CDs. "That's a Fender, an *American* Fender. It's worth a thousand dollars, if not more."

"Daniel, we're pawning it, not selling it."

"This is the best guitar that will ever come in here," he said, shutting the case. "Two hundred bucks is a joke. An insult. I'm sick." He tried to lift it off the counter. My hand came down on his arm.

"I want to talk to you," I growled. But the redhead leaned back and yelled up the staircase. "Bill-ee! I need you to come and look at this!"

I couldn't tell how old Billy was. Like the

street, he'd been fading for a long time. The stubble over his chin was salt-and-pepper gray but his hair, combed back and actually oiled, was black. He had knotted, sinewy arms like Daniel, but sunken cheeks buffed with high color, like Sy. A drinker's face.

It lit up when he opened the case. He looked at Daniel, his lips parted, pulling back in a smile.

"Yeah?" he said softly.

"Yeah," Daniel agreed. Billy lifted the guitar tenderly out of the case and positioned his foot on a chair to balance the pearl-plated body over his thigh. He plucked softly, expertly at the strings. The dull sound meant nothing to me; an electric guitar unplugged is a dead thing. But he seemed to be listening to something else.

"You're one shit-hot guitar man if this is yours," Billy said to Daniel. "Rock 'n' roll?"

"Blues," my brother said proudly.

Billy plucked a little riff, a series of notes that struck a chord even in my memory, from one of Daniel's tapes.

My brother's face was shining. "Basin Street."

"How much, Billy?" the woman interrupted.

"Oh..." The man sighed, as if the money was a painful thought. "Three fifty...seventy-five. Yeah, make it three seventy-five. Give him too much to come back."

The woman pulled out a pawn slip. "It's five

percent for thirty days, plus a holding fee. Press hard. You're making three copies."

While I filled out the slip, she wrote on a smaller green form, glancing up at me from time to time. I realized she was writing down a description of me.

"Police ticket," she explained. "It's the law. Everything that goes through pawn goes to the police."

I felt a flush of heat, a reminder that tomorrow was Sunday and after that was Monday and I still didn't know exactly what I was going to do about the truck. I wanted to be out of this place.

Billy was counting out the money to Daniel. "Be back in a month, guitar man, or *I'll* buy it. She'll be my baby," he said.

Daniel folded the money over without looking at it and stuffed it into his back pocket. He was smiling at the stringy, oiled guy like he was a friend.

"I thought I was your baby," the woman said to Billy, running her hand slowly up his arm, teasing but not. He looked at her the way he'd looked at the guitar, eyes that could bend metal with their heat.

I felt like cardboard.

"Let's go," I barked at Daniel. I tried to stride away but got stopped by the security gate; they had to buzz me out.

Walking to the truck, I did mental math. I'd always been good at it and sometimes I used it as a distraction if I was worried or bored. Standing on the lot of Five Star Ford, I'd figured out my commission on every vehicle there, based on the sticker price, at least once. Today, though, the work was for real.

"Okay, five percent of 375 is about nineteen bucks, plus the holding fee means that we'll have to pay around 410 to get the Fender back. Now, if we're selling the tapes for 7.95..."

"They're supposed to be ten dollars," Daniel cut in.

"We have to move these things. It's a price point – everybody wants a deal. I mean, maybe we'll start at ten but we'll go to eight, get it? Now, to pay off the guitar, it's about 50 tapes...51 actually. What do you owe Kruse? 4,850? Eight into forty-eight, that's...six...sixty."

The numbers seemed to hit me like a real thing, a tackle at 45 degrees, helmet blasting my ribs.

"That's over seven hundred tapes," I said softly. It was a lot, maybe even more than we had. I'd known this was going to be tough but to see that number chiseled in my mind made it huge, impossible. I didn't know how I'd do this in a month, never mind a week.

"We'll try for ten bucks," I whispered. I

cleared my throat and said it louder. "We're really going to try for ten."

We were at the truck. I unlocked the passenger side, then held out my hand.

"I'll hang onto the money," I said.

Daniel took a step back. "No."

I let go a short, irritated breath. "Don't do this now, okay? Just hand it over."

"No, I won't." His eyes were like dark, wet stones. "If you need it, you ask me. I'll give it to you."

The thought of my brother doling out money to me made me physically ill. "You're not going to walk around with four hundred bucks..."

"Yes, I am! Because you don't care. It's just money to you. It's my guitar."

The frustration seemed to burst in my chest, more than I knew was there. "I am so sick of hearing that. Will you get over it, already? The goddamn thing is gone, you're in shit up to your eyeballs, so let's just get on with it. Give me the money!"

I seized his arm to let him know I meant it, but I must have gripped him hard.

"Come on, hit me, Jens."

"Oh, shut up." I grabbed his jacket front with my other hand, to make him look at me.

"You want to be the big man? So do it."

"Daniel..."

"Hit me!"

The burning rush of strength was scaring me. I could have lifted him off the ground like a rag doll. I pushed him away.

Across the street at the bus stop, people were staring. I stalked around to the driver's door but before I opened it, I pointed at him.

"I have never hit you." My hand quivered. "I never will."

His nose was running, fear or fury or both.

"Wipe your face," I said, and swung into the truck.

He got in, rubbing his sleeve across his upper lip. I pulled my provincial road map out from behind the visor and tossed it at him.

"You want to call the shots? Go ahead. You figure out where we go, what we do. I don't care."

I fired up the engine and sat, waiting, staring straight ahead like a chauffeur. Daniel opened the map that seemed to fill the whole cab, crackling and rustling until I thought I would scream. But I didn't say a word.

"Okay," he said finally. "Let's get on Highway 51. We'll hit Starling first, do that tonight. It's on the way to Easton."

EIGHT

"Sales is about numbers," Sy had told me. "Ten prospects will get you one test-drive. Ten drives will get you one sale. The smart salesman says thank you to the customer who says no, because then he's one step closer to his next commission."

I had just started at Five Star Ford and this was part of my training. I wrote it down because I wrote down everything Sy said.

He looked out the window. "You can't take rejection personally. It's not about you. You're not asking the customer if he wants *you*."

Later I found out that he always gave the same speech to trainees; it was a song everybody knew the words to. Dave and I would practice late into the evening, the table cluttered with empties, the barroom blurred around the edges.

"Thank you – you stupid prick."

"No, no! Thank you, asswipe, for walking onto this lot and jerking me around..."

"Because your own life is so screwed..."

"You've got nobody to piss on but salesmen!"

We'd laugh till we almost cried.

When I made my first sale, we went to the same bar. Even late in the day I could still hardly believe it. I kept living it over and over, from the touchdown moment of *Yes*, to the golden flow that swept me through the paperwork and financing, to the final handshake that felt like the grip of a friend. Offer accepted. The money seemed like a bonus.

It wasn't enough to send home, but it was enough to celebrate with. I bought drinks for everybody. I tried to buy a drink for the waitress but she was on duty. After last call she came back to us – me and Dave and a few friends I'd made over the evening.

"Which one of you won the lottery?" she teased, and the warm weight of her as she settled on my knee felt like a prize. They were turning the lights out around us but we owned that table somehow. I was swimming in perfume and beer, that Yes handshake still tingling in my strong arm. Dave lifted his glass to me one more time.

"I knew you'd make it, you pushy S.O.B.," he said cheerfully. "Now you've got the taste in your mouth. You'll be all right."

And in that moment I understood why I was there, instead of unloading trailers or any other job. Because it wasn't about numbers. It was personal. I clinked Dave's mug with mine.

"I'll be all right now," I said.

◆

I pushed the speed limit all the way to Starling. There was no snow on this side of Winnipeg, either, except in the darkest shadows. The day that had started out pale and warm grew hot inside the truck. I squirmed out of my jacket and got stuck halfway, shaking and shaking my right sleeve that wouldn't come off. Finally Daniel grabbed the cuff and pulled, and I almost shuddered with relief.

"Thanks," I said gruffly, even though I wasn't speaking to him.

I was trying to figure out what radio station would bug him the most. My brother has an almost physical reaction to music – sixties soda pop rock can raise goosebumps on his arms, like nails on a blackboard does to other people. I have seen him become queasy in elevators and stores because of the synthesized music. I'd say it was an act, just one more thing he does to be strange, to drive me crazy, but I've seen it my whole life. When he was three, the TV commercial for a certain burger chain – with a dancing bear and a deep, bouncing tuba – would send him running from the room with his hands over his ears. And that was when some people still thought he was deaf.

The truck had a cassette deck but the only tape I had was Daniel's demo that he'd given me at Christmas. I'd never played it. My excuse was that I'd heard most of the eight songs – relentlessly – up through the damned vent in my room. My Christmas present was still in the glove box where I'd stuffed it, face down.

We were almost at Starling but I was watching the countryside, counting farms and wondering if anybody drove into town on a Saturday afternoon. Daniel was slumped against his door, beaten by the sappy love-song station I'd finally picked. When we got to the town limits he sat up and unrolled the window, as if he was gulping air.

Starling wasn't as big as Ile-des-Sapins. Main Street was *the* street, a handful of stores strung up both sides of the highway: a farm implement dealer, a hardware, a bank, the Times Change Cafe (featuring twelve kinds of pie), Darcy's Secondhand Fashions and a tiny Legion Hall. I had my own ideas about where to try, but I kept my mouth shut and drove slowly past the angled-in trucks and the few pedestrians sauntering along in the sun. No one even looked at us. Starling was built on the highway — all cars were strange cars.

We were nearly at the end of main street when Daniel turned to me.

"Here?" he said.

"Sure." I swung into the first free spot, in front of Darcy's and across from the Legion. I pulled out the keys and sat there, hands on my thighs.

Daniel glanced in the sideview mirror. "Maybe we should try the Legion? It's Saturday night. People will go there to drink. Maybe we should try to set something up?"

"Sure," I said, but I didn't move. Daniel waited, watching me, then began to fidget.

"What do you think, Jens?"

"I told you — sure. Go for it."

He finally yanked on the door handle and pushed his way out. I followed, biting the inside of my cheek to keep from smiling.

Legion Halls are not night clubs, or even bars. They may have other uses but in rural Manitoba they were built so ex-servicemen would have somewhere to get drunk as cheaply as possible. As private clubs, they don't serve the general public. There hasn't been a war in awhile, so most of the people who go to a Legion are pretty old.

Daniel was waiting for me outside the door. I gestured him in ahead, making him go first. After the brilliant sunshine of the street, the dim room struck me blind and for moments I just stood, blinking, unable to move in case I bumped into something.

The tail end of a conversation seemed to float out to me in the darkness.

"He's eighty-five years old, for God's sake. We have to do something — streamers, a cake?"

When my eyes adjusted, I saw about fifteen small round tables squeezed into one half of the room. The other half was dominated by a snooker table, a beautiful old giant in green felt and burnished wood. The fake panneled walls were hung with pictures, rows and rows of young soldiers. In the corner was a bar with a padded vinyl edge — bright orange-red, a color that somebody had gotten a deal on, for sure.

Three people were huddled at the bar — two men and a woman — staring at us. The Legion wasn't open yet. We wouldn't have been welcome even if it was.

"Can I help you, boys?" the woman behind the bar said. She was younger than the men, but her husky frame and short haircut reminded me of every mom who came out to cheer at a Rosetown Raiders game, or volunteered at the canteen.

Daniel glanced back at me expectantly. I smiled and said nothing. That's when he realized I wasn't going to take over, that he'd have to speak for himself. He looked at the woman, then back at me, lips parted in alarm.

"What do you boys want?" It was a demand but I could hear the fear in her voice. Was this a robbery? One of the men stood up, the larger one, a gray-dusted farmer with lined, leather skin and big shoulders.

"This is a private club," he said. "You have to leave."

"Do...do you ever have entertainment?" Daniel said in a breathy voice, as if he was squeezing the words out. "I mean, like, performers?"

"No." The farmer was looking at me. I was bigger and obviously more dangerous.

"Well, would you want to sometime? Like...tonight?"

"No," the farmer said. "Why would we?"

Daniel was rocking nervously, even as he clung to his ground.

"I'm a guitarist. Blues. I do shows and things, and I have a tape." He stuck his hands in his pockets defiantly. "I'm pretty good."

"I'm sure you are," the mother in the group said. "But we already have something planned for tonight. Sorry." She smiled, to soften it.

Daniel's back was to me but I could see him wilt. "Well...yeah. Okay. Maybe next time."

He turned for the door, his face pale from the strain.

I caught him by the shoulders. I'd been determined to let him fail but I couldn't stand it.

"Whose birthday is it?" I called.

The three at the bar looked back, faintly surprised that we hadn't left yet. Finally the second man cleared his throat.

"Jake Reimer. He's my uncle."

I headed toward them casually, my arm still on Daniel's back as I pushed him along with me. "Did I hear you say he's eighty-five? He must be one of the original homesteaders."

"The same year as the railroad," the man said proudly.

"We try to do that in Ile-des-Sapins, too," I said. "Celebrate the people who really built the town. It's easy to forget them sometimes."

"You're from Ile-des-Sapins?" the farmer said. The name was on his lips like a password. It was a small town, like their own.

"Yes, sir." I was close enough now, and I put my hand out to him. "Jens Friesen, and this is my brother, Daniel."

"Friesen!" the woman exclaimed. "Any relation to Dietrich and Mary? They're over in Sunnyhill."

This was a touchy point. I knew for a fact that my dad's relatives had moved to Saskatchewan.

I grinned. "Probably. There are so many of us, I'm sure we're all related somehow. 'Them that ain't Friesen is Froese.'"

It was an old joke but they grinned anyway, liked it better, maybe, because they had heard it so many times.

Daniel shifted restlessly. I knew he couldn't understand why I was still talking to these people; they'd already said no. I touched the back of his jacket again, telling him to wait.

I slid onto one of the bar stools. "So, what are you going to do for Jake?" I asked.

Not enough, according to his nephew. The birthday had been remembered at the last minute and the three of them were scrambling for ideas to make the old man's regular Saturday night trip to the Legion a bit festive.

"Well, it's lucky we got here today, then," I said. I told them my brother was a recording artist and we were traveling through the province promoting his debut release. It was the truth, only stretched out and shaped a bit.

"Recording artist? He looks just like my Kurt when he was in high school. You remember how skinny he was," the woman said to the farmer.

Daniel's muscles tensed, his chin went up. He was ready to leave right then. I started slapping my jacket pockets.

"You know, I meant to bring you in a tape, but I must have forgotten it. Daniel, run out to the truck and get one, please?"

He gave me a look — he was finished with these people. But he strode out anyway. As soon as the door shut, I leaned forward.

"His producers are really excited about him, his talent," I said in a low voice. My audience leaned in, too. "But he's so young. That's why we're building the exposure slowly, at a grass roots level."

The farmer arched an eyebrow at me. "Starling is grass roots?"

"Well, it's *wheat*," I said. Their chuckles encouraged me. "This is the big tour," I continued. "All the performers want to do Starling, Treehern, Portage la Prairie. After that, it's all downhill. You might as well do Vegas."

They burst into laughter, and it rolled over me like applause. A blinding flash lit up the dusty hall as Daniel came in. He walked up suspiciously, as if we were laughing at him, and tossed the tape at me. I caught it and gallantly handed it to the woman. The others crowded around to see.

"Blue Prairie, Daniel Desrochers," the

woman read out loud, then looked up at me. "He's your brother? I thought you said your name was Friesen."

My stomach clenched, the way it had when I'd first seen the tape at Christmas.

"It's my mother's maiden name," Daniel started. "It —"

He was going to say "sounds better" but I cut him off. "There...there's another Friesen who records...jazz." This was a real lie. A wave of nausea swept through me. "We don't want to confuse anyone."

The tape was working magic. The cover of Blue Prairie was a black-and-white art photo of Daniel with the Fender in a wheat field, his face so shadowed by his hat you couldn't tell how old he was, the field around him tinted blue. I had to hand it to Kruse — the package was professional.

"Now, that doesn't look a thing like Kurt," the woman said with a self-conscious laugh; I could tell she was impressed. The nephew was watching us hopefully now, but I was facing the farmer.

I knew the moment had come. *Ask*, Jens. Ask for the sale.

"I think my brother could put on a good show for you," I blurted. I could have kicked myself — it was a statement, not a close. The farmer looked Daniel up and down, still cautious. The words bubbled up nervously inside me — how Daniel could play anything, how thrilled Jake would be — but I bit it back. After the pitch you have to wait for the swing.

"We couldn't afford to pay him, not really," the farmer said at last.

"For Jake," I said, "Daniel would be happy to do it."

By the time I reached the sidewalk I was flying. I'd done it! We had a real booking. I felt the first rush of hope I'd had in a long time. I decided to take Daniel to the Times Change, get a coffee and make a plan.

"Well, thanks a lot," my brother said. "I love doing shows for nothing, especially for shit-boot farmers who wouldn't know good music if it bit them on the ass."

My mood hit the ground and didn't even bounce. "What's the matter with you? Weren't you listening? Everybody in town will turn up for this old guy. We'll have a captive audience. And if it weren't for me, you wouldn't even have that. You'd be on the sidewalk with your case open, begging."

"It's busking," he muttered, hands in his pockets. "It's an art."

I'd never had the stomach to watch my brother do it. It always struck me as...desperate.

"Well, not in Starling," I said. "Believe me, a freebie at the Legion is the best you're going to get, tonight or maybe any night. You're lucky, you know that?"

I was gearing up for a lecture — how ungrateful he was, how he never appreciated what people did for him. *Desrochers* was still lodged inside me like a bullet. My brother didn't care at all about the only thing that mattered to me.

"Yeah, I'm lucky, Jens," Daniel said quietly. "You're so smooth. Everybody likes you and...you can get anything. But you know, you never even told them I was any good."

He sounded so hungry. It took me a moment to speak, but when I managed it, my voice was light.

"I did, too. Didn't you hear me in there? I said you could put on a good show." I pushed open the door to the Times Change. "Buy me some pie, Daniel?"

NINE

We got great table service in the cafe. The waitress was about Daniel's age and she came by every few minutes to check my coffee.

"Refills are free," she said, grinning at me. Her blonde hair was tied back in a ponytail but strands had come loose, brushing her pink cheeks.

Daniel was watching me, dark-eyed. At another table, a group of girls – probably the waitress's friends – were watching, too.

"What do I get if I pay for it?" I teased, loud enough for them to hear. They whooped into sudden laughter. The waitress twisted around, scarlet, to make faces at them. My brother looked away.

When it was time to leave, she gave me the bill and hurried back to her giggling friends. At the bottom she'd drawn a heart with a happy face on it, and written, *Have a great day! My name is Marcy. Come back SOON.*

I passed it to Daniel with a smile — he was paying. He glanced at it, then crumpled it up. He left the money on the table.

Out on the sidewalk, I couldn't resist elbowing him. "You didn't leave Marcy much of a tip."

"Leave your own goddamn tip," Daniel muttered.

The man at the Petro-Canada service station told us there was a rest stop about three kilometers beyond Starling. It turned out to be a half-moon of gravel with two picnic tables on it.

Daniel kicked at the ground, scattering stones. "This is nuts. Why can't we sleep in the truck?"

"Because we'd have to unload it to make room," I said irritably. "You want your guitars to sit out on the highway all night, for whoever wants to pick them up?"

The truth was, with the Fender gone, I could have squeezed out a narrow aisle through the stuff, enough room for Daniel and me to lie with our backs touching, or to sleep like spoons, the way we did when we were really small and there was a thunderstorm. Lots of kids don't like thunder but for Daniel, who was even frightened of that burger bear's tuba, it was the end of the world. I remember him pulled in against me, his breath on my back, wincing at every crack and boom. I was always on the outside edge, so that whatever horror was coming in that terrible sound would have to get me first.

But we weren't those kids anymore. I would sooner have died than sleep with my brother.

We'd passed a copse of trees on the way out, and I drove back to it. There wasn't a farmhouse as far as I could see but I knew we were on somebody's land. I felt a guilty pang as Daniel and I unloaded, but if we set up the tent by the picnic tables, in full view from the highway, it might not be there when we got back from the Legion.

The tent was an army green that blended into the brush quite well, even though most of it was still leafless. Setting up camp took us an hour and a half and I was glad – anything to keep my mind from running anxiously to the night ahead.

I was as nervous as hell. I wanted to get to the Legion early, to meet people as they came in. I had a big job ahead of me – there's a difference between what people will clap for and what they'll buy.

Remember FAB, I told myself. It was a buzzword that meant Features, Advantages, Benefits – a progression to lead the customer through to the sale. "It doesn't matter what you're selling," Sy said. "Cars or toasters or whatever. Product is product. The process is the same."

My product was playing to the trees. He'd lugged the acoustic out of the truck and was turned away from me, the amp under him as a seat. He wasn't really playing, only strumming, hard bursts over the strings, his left hand leaping up and down the neck of the guitar. It wasn't completely tuneless but it was aggravating. He had a show to do tonight. Why didn't he practice a song or something?

Don't fight, I told myself. Just make dinner.

I dug out a large can of ravioli and started fooling around with the propane stove. I'd never used one before but how tough could it be? Crouched in front of it, I kept easing open the fuel gauge and tried match after match until I was cursing under my breath. What could be wrong? Dad said he'd filled the tank.

The violent strumming was getting to me.

"What is that noise?" I said.

"They're power chords," he said, not missing one.

"Well, it sucks. Why don't you think about what you're going to play tonight?" Maybe the line from the tank to the burner was clogged.

"I am. This is how I think."

I cranked the throttle wide open. "Most people think with their brains, Daniel," I said, and thrust the match into the burner.

The gust of ignition blew me backwards onto my ass.

There was a half-second of silence, then Daniel began to laugh. Then I began to laugh. We blurted it out at the same instant: *"Scheisskopf!"*

We sounded so much like Dad that it set us off again, giggling like drunks.

It was Daniel who suggested that if we ate out of the can we wouldn't have to wash any dishes.

It was nearly seven o'clock when he crawled into the tent with his performance clothes to get changed. He'd always been shy like that. I emptied out one of my duffle bags in the truck and filled it with tapes. I made sure I had over a hundred, but in my heart I only needed to sell twenty. Salesmen have magic numbers and tonight this one was mine. If I could sell twenty tapes, that would be a sign – that this would work, that I could do it.

I changed my sweatshirt to something neater. "When you stand in front of a customer, you have to look like you don't need the money," Sy said. Daniel came up, denim shirt hanging outside his jeans, leather vest open. But I didn't say a word. He had a show to do and the better he played, the more tapes we'd sell. He was my product and I had to pump him up.

"This is great," I said as we drove to Starling. "This is a real chance and they're dying to hear you. Don't worry about anything. You just get out there and play your best and I'll do everything else."

It was full darkness now and I could feel new energy running through me. There is something exciting about the prairie at night. The surrounding fields are oceans of black, magnifying every headlight. The storefronts of a place like Starling can look like Times Square.

The front of the Legion was already lined with vehicles, so we parked farther down the street. I didn't mind — cars meant customers. I was eager to get started when Daniel grabbed his fedora off the dashboard.

"For Pete's sake, don't wear the hat," I snapped.

"Why not?"

"Because...it's strange. People want you to look like them."

"But I'm not like them," he said defiantly.

"Couldn't you fake it for just one night?"

He swung around to look at me, the bones of his lean face strong in the light of the cafe.

"I love this hat. It's my signature. If people don't like it, that's their problem."

"Oh, *that* attitude is going to sell tapes."

Daniel stuck the fedora firmly on his head. "Not my job, Jens. You just said so. All I've got to do is play. Well, this is how I play."

He pushed out. I thumped the steering wheel with the heel of my hand. But as I unloaded the equipment, I said, "At least tuck in your shirt. You look like a poster boy for Child Find."

He didn't speak to me the long walk up to the hall.

The Legion was busy but not yet full. The walls were scalloped with streamers—green and red, orange and black, leftovers from both Christmas and Halloween. Five men were at the snooker table, two teams plus one grizzled consultant, and the tables were either clustered or completely empty. No one sat alone. There were wives and mothers scattered through the crowd, but this was a place of men. Work pants and blue jean jackets, smoke and beer.

Word must have gotten around that we were coming. When we walked in, the room seemed to dip, conversations changed direction. Everyone looked, yet I knew it wasn't at me. I was just a stranger. Daniel was a *kid*, with two guitars. I grinned hello to every face that would meet mine. Daniel strode up to the bar as if the place was empty.

The farmer we'd met that afternoon was

named Allan Rutley. He was leaning against the padded ledge of the bar, twirling a toothpick anxiously in his mouth. I shouldered past Daniel to get to him first.

"Well, here we are," I said. "Hope we're not late."

"No," Rutley said. He was staring at the two-foot amplifier I was struggling to balance. Daniel promptly set down his guitars at the table closest to the wall, shrugged off his jacket and began setting up.

"Could I get you to move?" he said to a nearby table of three men. "I need some room here."

I heard the grumble, and the discontented scraping of chairs. Rutley glanced back at them.

"You...you did a great job with the decorations," I said quickly as I set down the amp. "Jake is going to be thrilled."

"Look," Rutley said, stepping closer. "How loud is he going —"

"Do you have a microphone?" Daniel cut in.

The man looked at him as if he were a bug. "No. Why would we?"

Daniel snorted, soft but unmistakable. "Right. Why would you." He turned away, too fast. Rutley raised an eyebrow at me. I could feel the sweat gathering under my arms and around my collar.

"Allan," I said, easing him away, "let me buy you a beer."

I left some of my gas money on the bar, then swept in beside Daniel, as if I was helping him.

"Get a personality," I hissed, "or I'll drive your ass back home tonight, I swear to God."

I couldn't see his face but he hesitated; the brim of the fedora quivered.

I built a pyramid of cassettes for display on the table, and took some in my hand. As Daniel slung the strap of the electric guitar over his shoulder and began to tune up, I looked at the crowd.

Cold calls, any salesman will tell you, are the hardest. It takes guts to start at zero, come face to face with someone who didn't ask for what you have to sell. There weren't a hundred people in the Legion, not even fifty yet, but I could tell by the backs and shoulders turned against us, these were all cold calls. I took a deep breath and waded in.

"Hi, how are you tonight?" I began over and over as I moved through the room. I tried to work in the important things quickly: the Friesen name, the fact that we were from Ile-des-Sapins, and that we were doing this for Jake.

"Would you know him if you saw him?" one woman asked point-blank. The truth paralyzed me for a few seconds before I managed to laugh nervously and tell her it was the thought that counted. I tried not to slink away.

Every table I stopped at, I showed Daniel's tape. Some people glanced at it in curiosity but most had only one question: Was he old enough to be in here? I had to keep explaining that as long as he didn't drink and as long as I was with him as a guardian, it was legal. But that wasn't the same as welcome. The magic twenty tapes seemed as impossible as seven hundred.

One man in a crisp white shirt and a heavy gold watch leaned over the snooker table and sank the pink with a decisive crack. "Does your brother play that thing or does he just tune it?" he said.

At that instant the room burst into sound, electric vibration, notes running wild, not up and down the scale but around it and through it. I looked. Everyone did. I'd never heard this song before, not on one of Daniel's CDs, not floating up through my bedroom vent. It was pure instrumental – I couldn't imagine words keeping up with it. If this was R & B, it was that music on drugs, blues at 150 kilometers an hour.

Daniel wasn't looking at us. Head down, brim hiding his face, he was watching the fingers of his left hand fly over the frets. My mind leapt back to Mickey's pawn shop. One shit-hot guitar man. He deserved that Fender.

Climbing the scale, dropping, then climbing again, dancing on it, until suddenly it was over. There was a moment of stunned silence, then the feeling came up through my chest, a rush of awe. I started to clap. The room abruptly joined in, and Daniel looked up shyly. His bare sixteen-year-old face was a shock to me. I'd forgotten this was my brother. But he was surprised, too, as if he couldn't believe it was me out there, clapping so hard.

The whole night wasn't like that, but it set the tone. It was a good thing. Daniel was a brilliant guitarist, but he had utterly no talent with an audience. He was playing only instrumentals and he hid behind his hat. People asked *me* for requests. One man, drinking fast, desperately wanted to hear the Animals' classic, House of the Rising Sun. When I passed it on, Daniel rolled his eyes as if I'd just asked him to spend the morning in kindergarten. I had to go back later and lay it out plainly for him.

"This guy has three nephews and he'll buy a tape for each of them if you just play the damn song. But if you don't do it soon, he's going to be too pissed to get his wallet out."

That did it. Daniel started off snarky, too fast, but he got lost in the beauty of that old song, the haunting melody of a ruined life. For a second time the room seemed to stop, transfixed. Daniel wasn't singing but it didn't matter. The fast drinker knew the words and he was mouthing them or singing softly, the rims of his eyes suddenly bright. Everyone from Starling seemed to understand whose song this was and why.

On the very last quavering note, Uncle Jake the birthday man walked in, and the room leapt to its feet in a standing ovation – for him, for the fast drinker, for Daniel. My brother rolled into Happy Birthday, full of electric riffs, and the applause went on and on. The old man had to sit down; he kept touching his hand to his temple. He might have been expecting something but not quite this: music and streamers and a roomful of people drunk with gratitude and love.

"Jens, buy me a beer."

Daniel was taking a break, resting up for the second set. I was touching base, hovering like a coach. I wanted him to loosen up and talk to the audience.

"I'll get you a pop," I said.

"No, I want to sing. I need a beer."

"We'll get kicked out..." I argued.

"By who? They love me here."

I saw my mother's worried face, but it seemed long ago and far away. And Daniel was right. They did love him, and they loved me, too. I was rushing on a salesman's high, the thrill of people glad to see me, wanting what I had to offer. The money was growing thicker in my wallet and nudging me from behind. I knew I was nearing my magic number, and I didn't want it to stop.

"Just one," I told him. I bought a beer and got a glass, and shielded behind him I filled it slowly and at an angle, so it wouldn't foam. "If anybody asks, you say it's ginger ale," I said.

He took down a third of it in a single swallow, and I felt a dim pulse of concern. "I mean it, I'm not buying another," I said.

"Don't worry." He opened the case to the acoustic. I waded out into what was now a packed, smoky hothouse, determined to pick up the trail of money again.

There is magic in an acoustic guitar. Maybe it's the campfire memories or maybe it's just friendlier than an electric. Whatever the reason, once Daniel started singing, the room seemed to draw closer to him, wrap around him. People stopped asking me for songs, and started asking him.

I wasn't really listening. The music seemed to take place at the edge of my hearing. One song caught me, though, maybe because it was softer and slower, as pretty as a ballad. I was certain it was a request — my brother didn't write love songs. I think it was called Chantel.

I was too busy to listen long. Occasionally I'd look over and I was mystified. Daniel kept drinking but his glass never seemed to empty. Then I saw the snooker player in the white shirt sidle up to him, making a request. My brother smiled and touched his glass. The man smiled back and left his own full one on the table.

The little sneak! I felt an angry flare before reason took over. Give him hell tomorrow, I told myself. Tonight he's what they want.

Not since my days of chocolate almonds had I been on such a roll. I couldn't fold up the bills fast enough. But it wasn't just about money. I was hungry to talk to people, glad to listen to any life that wasn't my own. The stories and hushed secrets wrapped around me like an arm: the wife who gambled away the house; the daughter who ran off with her teacher. The memory of yesterday morning was easing away, and I needed it to. I needed somebody to trust me.

"This song is from my debut. I only sing it when I'm pissed."

Daniel's slurred voice leapt out at me across the smoky buzz. At the back of the room I stood up, straining to see him. He was sitting now, vest gone, sweat staining dark circles on the denim shirt. He was hugging the guitar, hat pushed back, his bleary face naked to the audience.

He wasn't just high, he was smashed.

Alarm shot through my body. Pack it up, get him out now.

"It's about the worst night of life," Daniel continued, and he grinned stupidly, bravely. "It's for my brother."

I was rooted to the floor. He struck the first chords and dimly I realized this was a ballad, too, but it was no love song.

All I ever did was walk behind you
Try to learn how to be
I guess you never asked for
A shadow who looked like me
You were there first
So I guess it's your right
To throw me out
Chew me up
Cut me down
But did you ever think...that was my room too?
You had lots of friends, I had only you
You had the whole world, I had that room
But, hey, it's your right

There was a sketching of applause. Some people glanced at me but it was late and many were too drunk to care.

I was sober. I sat down heavily, the room spinning, my guts churning.

TEN

It happened at the end of April in my grade nine year. I'd been fifteen for a week and I liked it. I was five-feet-eleven – not the tallest guy in my year, but the only one who could take down our gym teacher Mr. Flett in wrestling, take him down and keep him there, make him grunt and struggle, then finally laugh. He said he was glad I'd be going to Rosetown Senior High the next year.

"Yeah, Jens, that's how I keep my job," Mr. Flett teased. "Keep the boys home and send the men on to Rosetown."

I was feeling so close. I'd had my learner's permit for three months and I was doing really well – terrific, Mom said. That day in April she'd promised I could drive us to Winnipeg for dinner out; Dad was working late. Daniel could ride up front with me, and she'd sit in the back.

"I'll read a book," she said. "I won't say a word."

Daniel and I were revved about it. It was almost like being out on our own.

"Let's go to Gooey's for pizza subs," he said cheerfully. "She hates that place!"

"When I've got my license, you and me will go there all the time," I promised.

I had lots of plans for when I got my license.

In a small town, everybody dates everybody else eventually, although "date" is probably too complicated a word. The people I knew just hung around together. There were some basement parties, some school dances, some moments along the dark north wall of the rec center. But until you could drive there was hardly any way to be alone with someone you liked.

I liked Mona Perenthaler and I was pretty sure she liked me. In a group, we always wound up standing next to each other. Maybe I was kind of goofy and loud sometimes, but she laughed at my jokes. And when she talked, I shut up. I had experience with shy people; I knew you had to listen.

Part of me seemed to be listening to her all the time. I could lose my train of thought standing next to her, swept up by the nearness of her high, heavy breasts and long back, her curving buttocks that strained against the pockets of her jeans, exactly the same height as where my hands would be, if she was against me.

Mona was taller than many of the other girls but still she managed to look up at me, cheeks flushing pink, biting her lip in a way that made me want to bite it, too. Even in a crowd, I could almost hear her heart beat.

That afternoon in April I was excited by my life, barely able to squeeze my shoulders down the aisle of the bus that was taking us out for the Rosetown Introductory Field Trip.

R.I.F.T. was a tradition, and a joke. Because all the kids from the smaller towns went to Rosetown Senior, one day each spring they'd bring in the new groups for a tour — as if our families didn't shop in that town every week. But the real joke was the acronym. The open house probably did more to stir up rivalries than anything else they could have done. A small place like Floret might only have two or three students starting at a time. That year from Ile-des-Sapins we had twenty-two.

On the bus we seemed like more.

"For Pete's sake, tone it down!" Mr. Wiebe called back at us, time after time. But we were on our way into new territory. We needed to be bigger than we were; we needed to be more.

And Mona Perenthaler was on that bus. I couldn't tone it down.

If Rosetown had any sense, they would have given their own school the day off for this, but they didn't. And so as we were led around – the gym, the labs, the classrooms – there were moments when every high-school kid in the province seemed wedged into the same hallway.

By three o'clock we'd been in our coats too long. I was overheated and bored, the skin under my shirt itchy with sweat. Just as Mr. Wiebe was trying to lead our group out, the final bell rang. Doors burst open and the hallway flooded. "Stay together, people. Stay together!" Mr. Wiebe shouted, but I was shuffled back by the surge from all directions. All I wanted was to get out into the cold air, but I was trapped, waiting for an opening.

"Another Ile-des-Sapins bastard."

I turned to see Chris Butler. Big, brooding, pig-eyed, he was six feet tall in grade nine, the cousin of a friend of a friend, and he was from Floret. We'd played a pick-up game of football together last fall, on the same team. He couldn't run worth a damn, wouldn't even try, and I'd told him so.

I was in a bad mood, but I wasn't going to play his game today. I ignored him and tried to move ahead.

"Hey, Friesen. Ever ask your mom why she married your dad?"

The strange question caught me, made me look back against my will.

"Because Mennonites are so fucking stupid they believe babies take five months."

My face was suddenly burning. I took a step toward him, the school and my group fading away.

"I don't think I heard you right. In fact, I know I didn't."

I was big in that hallway. The walls seemed to be squeezing the breath out of me, but Chris was bigger and he held his ground.

"Then I'll keep it simple – French slut."

I hit him, exploded at him in a furious charge. We might have crashed into people on the way down but I didn't notice. If Chris landed me a few times, I didn't feel it.

It took three male teachers to drag us apart. The bus back to Ile-des-Sapins didn't wait for me. Before he left, Mr. Wiebe made sure I knew I had the rest of the week off – a suspension.

"I just can't believe this, not from you, Jens," he kept saying, mad and hurt at the same time. He didn't understand: there were things you didn't do to my family.

They tried to make us say how it started.

Sitting straight in my chair, fingers locked on my lap, I said I didn't remember.

"And what about you, Chris?"

He looked at me. My jacket was torn and the left side of my face had begun to sting with a scrape where he'd cuffed me good. But I wasn't afraid of him and I let him see it.

"I don't remember," Chris muttered.

While we were in the office, they phoned our homes for someone to come get us.

Please not Dad, I prayed. Self-control. I'd really blown it this time.

It was Mom who came, her pale skin even whiter than usual, dark hair pulled back, her delicate features looking sharp and awake. But she didn't make a fuss over my cut and she didn't cry. We got in the car and pulled onto the highway home.

"I'm sorry, I'm really sorry," I said, and I was. Not that I'd hit Chris, because I still felt he deserved it, but that I'd probably embarrassed her, made her come get me, given people something to gossip over.

"I want to know what that was about," Mom said.

I felt myself flush. There were things you never said to your mother, words you never used in front of her. But this was even worse than that.

"It was stupid," I said hurriedly. "It was nothing."

"People don't fight about nothing — or you don't."

"I don't want to talk about it, all right?!" I was getting mad. I was just trying to protect her.

My mother swung over onto the gravel shoulder, thrust the shift into park and put on the blinking hazard lights.

"Then we'll sit here until you do," she said simply.

For minutes we waited, engine idling. I shifted in the front seat, feeling huge and awkward. Why did she have to know? Why couldn't I just be punished? Underneath, it was more than that. I was fifteen. I thought about sex a lot. I talked about it a lot with my friends. But there's this mental circuit that keeps you from thinking about sex and your parents at the same time. It just seems so impossible.

And yet they were both in the car with me. The heat was on and my skin was curdling. I was trying to think of the least painful way out of this.

"Was it about you?" Mom said finally.

I shook my head.

"Was it about Daniel?"

"It was about Dad," I blurted. "Chris said that maybe he isn't...you know, my real dad." I grinned sheepishly and shrugged. "I know, it's so stupid. People will say anything to bug you. I don't usually pay attention to garbage but...he caught me by surprise. Pissed me off."

There was no sound except the engine, and the rush of a passing car. I was waiting for her to say something but she was looking at her hands.

"I'm really sorry," I finished. "It won't happen again."

"But you might hear it again," she said softly. "From other people." She looked at me, dark eyes clear and careful. "Jens, I had another... boyfriend. I had a few boyfriends, all at the same time," she started.

She talked about growing up in the town of Antelier with her sisters, four Catholic girls living with their silent mother, all under the watchful, possessive eye of their father, Gerard. Jewels in his crown, he called his daughters. He was so strict, so old-fashioned that people talked about it; even the priest told Gerard to lighten up.

There was no money for university, so each of the girls got a job right out of high school. But they still lived at home; their father wouldn't hear of anything else. The sisters took every opportunity to get out of the house. My mother said she wanted to be liked.

She got pregnant. Not a big deal for a twenty-year-old girl living anywhere else. My mother came home from work one day to find her clothes scattered over the front lawn. Gerard wouldn't give her a suitcase. He wouldn't even open the door. She had to ask a neighbor for plastic garbage bags to gather her things in.

"There was my winter coat, everything," Mom said. "It was too heavy to carry. I had to drag the bags down the street. I was so embarrassed I thought I was going to die."

She didn't know what else to do, so she took her things to the home of the kindest man she had dated, and told him the truth. She moved in and two months later they got married and moved to Ile-des-Sapins. Gerard never spoke to her again.

I was sick, the images swirling in front of me the way they do at a cliff edge. It must have been awful for her; it was awful for me now. I felt as if my whole life was falling back in a sudden, dizzying slide. I scrambled desperately after it, trying to grab the most important thing.

"Is he my father or isn't he?" I broke in.

"I don't know," she said.

"How couldn't you? Women know these things! You're the ones who tell us."

"Jens, you're upset..."

"There's tests," I said. "It's just blood, right? Dad and I could go to the doctor today..."

"He won't do it."

"Why not, for Christ's sake?!"

She grabbed my arm. "Listen! Listen to me. He loves you. This is his way of showing it, proving that it doesn't matter."

"It matters to me." I threw myself against the door and stumbled out, almost slid down into the snow-filled ditch. But I pulled myself up and started to walk.

The prairie spring wind blasted my coat open, traced icy fingers over my sweaty body. I marched on anyway. I felt like someone else, or some big animal lumbering forward, the rage and hurt gathering in my chest, rising up my throat into the two words I knew I shouldn't say.

But Chris Butler had been right. About everything.

"Jens! You are not walking home. Get in the car."

The passenger window was open. She was driving slowly along beside me, one hand on the wheel but leaning toward me, worried.

"I can't," I said. "Not yet."

The danger must have been in my face. She drew back just a bit. "All right. I'll meet you up ahead. But do up your coat. You're going to get sick."

It was too late, but I zipped my jacket obedi-ently. She watched me for a moment, then pulled onto the road again. She drove to a sign about half a kilometer ahead and stopped, waiting. My gaze fastened on the distant taillights beaming back at me like two red eyes.

I had always known how to want things. As a kid, I started getting ready for Christmas before Halloween, leafing through catalogs, poring over the brilliant photographs. I never had a big list; sometimes it was just one special thing. But I could get lost in time on that page, looking and wishing, my fingers leaving damp marks on the paper.

I had wanted my driver's license, and I wanted Mona Perenthaler. Late at night, the room dark and quiet except for Daniel's deep-sleep breathing and my own, faster and more feverish, wanting her in color and 3-D and stereo, wanting her so badly I could make it happen.

And it was all dust. On that cold, windy Manitoba highway in April, I realized that what I needed – all I'd ever wanted – was to be the son of the best man I knew.

I was shaking by the time I reached the car. A deep chill, I guess. The wind had pulled water from my eyes, streaked it over my face that was too cold to feel it.

I got inside.

"I don't want anyone to know," I said. "Don't tell Dad about today."

She hesitated, biting her lip.

"I'm not sure..."

"Yes, you can! I think you owe me."

She should have slapped me. I could hear the snotty tone in my voice but I couldn't stop it, any more than I could stop another resentment, like poison, brewing under my skin.

We drove home in silence. I heard the guitar as soon as I opened the back door. Daniel was playing it on his bed but he looked up when I walked in.

"What took you so long? I thought we were going to Gooey's. We're still going, right?"

"Get out," I said.

"What?"

"Get the fuck out of my room!"

He stood up, almost white with shock, still clutching the neck of the guitar. I never talked like this — not to him, not to anybody.

"Jens..."

"Right now!" I grabbed the guitar case and swung it roughly out into the hallway. I seized the pillow off his bed and threw it out after him. Then the quilt, then the sheets, balled up and pitched out.

"Mommm!" He went running to the kitchen and I heard their voices, fast and furious, in French. As always, I didn't know what they were saying but for the first time I didn't care.

They couldn't stop me. Books and models and his stack of *Guitar Now* magazines, everything that was my brother's littered the hallway in a hurricane sprawl. I had just carried out one of his dresser drawers when I saw him.

He was backed down the hallway, as close as he dared come, hands clenched into fists. But he was twelve years old and no match for me; neither of them were. Behind him in the light of the kitchen I could see my mother, arms wrapped around her waist as if she was holding herself up. Daniel was so mad I don't think he knew he was crying.

"You can't do this, Jens. That's my room, too!"

I flipped the drawer, socks and shirts tumbling onto the pile. Then I turned inside and shut him out.

"I never did anything to you." Yelling at me through the door, hoarse with hurt disbelief. "I never did anything!"

There was a cassette in my tape player and I turned it on and up, loud. I fell onto my bed and squeezed the pillow around my face. It caught the sound that tore out of me, the sound of me ripping apart. I wasn't the man I'd wanted so badly to be. But Daniel was, or he would be. No matter what he grew up into, he'd always be sure of who he was. And I didn't hate him. I just couldn't bear the sight of him.

And he wasn't the only one. I'm sure Mona Perenthaler never understood what happened, how I could go from hot to cold in one afternoon. There would be other girls, eventually, but it would never be the same. I'd left that part of me on the highway. It wasn't Mona's fault but I couldn't tell her.

Somewhere in the dark I made myself a promise. I decided I couldn't prove I was my father's child but I could deserve it. I could earn it. If I tried hard and kept trying, I could be something.

I just needed it to happen fast.

ELEVEN

I woke up hurting, my muscles raw from a night on the ground. It had been a long time since I'd slept in a tent. Every part of me that wasn't burrowed inside the sleeping bag was chilled right through, even though I was still in my clothes. But I didn't try to go back to sleep. I rolled up onto my elbow to look at my brother.

We were so close that our sleeping bags almost lapped over each other. Daniel's dark hair was a mess and he was still in his clothes, too. I had a few inches and fifty pounds on him, but last night it had been all I could do to get him from the truck to the tent, a flashlight in one hand and holding him up with my other arm. Now, in the dim light, he seemed old, the morning's beard like a shadow on his skin.

I was scared. Last night wasn't a good time

that had slipped over the edge. He'd been drinking at a dead run, as much as he could get, as
fast as he could get it. The edge was the goal.

A tight band around my chest was squeezing
the breath out of me. I knew I should take him
home right away, tell Mom she was right, and
admit I didn't know what to do. Except I was
afraid Dad had been right, too. Daniel's problems were my fault. I struggled with the panic,
like drowning.

You can't fix it, Jens. You can't take back four
years.

But I could make it up to him. I could sell
seven hundred tapes; I'd already sold thirty-five.
I'd beaten my last night's goal by seventy-five
percent, and if I was just smarter and tried harder I could do it. I had to do it.

I remembered the money, the 375 dollars
from the Fender. There was no way Daniel
should be hanging onto it now. I should have
slipped it away from him last night, just to prove
to him how easy it was to lose, especially in that
condition. It occurred to me that the lesson
might still work.

My brother was lying on his back. I shrugged
off my sleeping bag and crept over, shivering a
little. It seemed so sneaky.

You're not stealing anything, I told myself.
You're just proving a point.

Crouched on my knees, I nudged his left shoulder, gently at first, then firmer. Success! Daniel rolled up onto his side, the sleeping bag riding with him. I leaned over him and reached down into the warm cocoon, carefully groping for his wallet.

His head twisted back suddenly, eyes squinting into mine.

"What the hell are you doing?"

I had to think fast. I pressed on his stomach, in the vicinity of his bladder.

"Time to get up!"

"Jens!" He jack-knifed to protect himself, his legs hitting the side of the tent so hard he yanked out one of the bearing poles and collapsed the whole thing down on us. The next few seconds were pandemonium – Daniel swearing, thrashing to get out. Me laughing and then desperate to get out, too, because now I had to go. It was like trying to beat our way out of a plastic bag, blindfolded. We made it just in time.

The morning was overcast, gray-white sky stretching forever in all directions over endless brown fields. I could see my breath. Back at our deflated tent, I realized Daniel was shaking and so was I.

"J-J-Jesus, it's cold!"

We bolted for the truck. Luckily I had the

keys in my pants pocket. I cranked the engine and we each folded in on ourselves, trying to stay warm until the heat kicked in. Daniel was rocking a little, rubbing his arms.

"We're going to die," he said, curled in so tight his chin was on his chest. "It's not worth it. We're going to freeze to death."

"We made 280 dollars last night," I said.

He looked at me, pure astonishment.

"Get out! Really?"

"Thirty-five tapes at eight bucks each." I couldn't keep the pride from my voice.

"So now he thinks he's good," Daniel said, smiling faintly. The heat had begun to work and he thrust his hands in front of it. "But it should have been 350. I thought you were going to ask for ten."

The jab stung. I wanted to shoot back that he hadn't been worth it. Drunk, he was only an eight-dollar man. But this morning I'd been thinking about all the days I couldn't take back.

"Introductory offer," I said.

"You make me sound like a product," Daniel sniffed.

"Well, you are. We all are. Those people didn't know us. They only knew what we showed them, the package."

Daniel was rubbing his hands. "I guess I wasn't much of a package. I guess I got kind of...tanked."

I hesitated. He was just across the seat but he seemed so far away from me.

"I'm worried about you," I said quietly.

"Don't try to be Dad, Jens," he said, crossing his arms over his chest. "And don't tell me you never..."

"Yeah, I want to have a good time, too. But I know a lot of people. And the ones who drink like that, who are going at it to *get* pissed, they're not doing it because it's fun."

"So I need a boost. You don't know what it's like to go out there, just you in front of everybody..."

"I do so," I said. "I go out in front of customers – strangers – all the time."

"But it's not *you* on the line. You're selling something else. It's not personal."

The heat came to my face. I could feel my heart.

"When I'm up there, they're judging me," he said.

"So why do it?" I said. "Who says you have to perform? A lot of songwriters never get up on stage. Why do something that's...painful?"

For a minute there was only the sound of the heater, warm air blowing in the truck cab.

"It's like rain, you know. The way it sounds. It starts off soft, just a few people clapping, and then it pours down like a thunderstorm. And it fills you up."

I didn't know what to say. He was telling me something I understood. He was telling me about Yes, and that he needed it, like I did.

But I couldn't admit it. I was older; I was supposed to be...stronger.

At last Daniel's mouth curled into a grin. "Maybe I just need to be vacuum-packed."

"What?"

"For freshness. I'm the product, right? We'll get those little stickers." He gestured, as if pinning them onto his body. "On sale! Buy now! In-store special!"

I laughed with relief. "No, think cars. Put a flag on your aerial."

"Put a flag on your own aerial!"

"Nah, a bestseller you don't have to advertise."

"Oh, make me puke!" He shoved me but he was laughing. "'I'm Marcy. Do you want a refill? Come back soon!'"

We just got stupid for awhile. By the time we tumbled out to pack up the camp, we were thoroughly awake, limbs warm and loose.

It didn't take long. Inside the truck again, I looked him over.

"Okay, you need a shower," I said. "And to shave."

"You, too!"

"And you can't wear that shirt again unless we find a laundromat. And we need to phone Mom and Dad, tell them we're going to..." I gestured at the glove box. "Pull out the map."

"Easton," Daniel said, without moving.

The engine was already running, but I twisted in my seat to look at him.

"Who's in Easton? Tell me."

"Somebody."

"Come on, tell me!"

"It's a girl, okay? I just want to go there."

Daniel and a girl. I was amazed. As far as I knew, he'd never dated anyone. He was shy even with the kids in Ile-des-Sapins, the ones we'd known all our lives. But maybe that was it; in a small town people seem to know you before you're born. And the labels they stick on you, like autistic or deaf or strange, enter a room before you ever do.

"I don't know anything about Easton," I started. "How big it is, or what's there."

I shifted into reverse, backed a half-circle as I aimed for the highway. "So I guess we'd better go see it."

Daniel didn't answer. He was watching me cautiously, as if he expected me to change my mind. The truck bounced over the rough little trail and then up onto the pavement.

"But first, moneybags, you're going to buy me a cup of coffee," I said lightly. Daniel hesitated, still watching me. From the corner of my eye I saw him arch off the seat to get his wallet out of his back pocket.

"You don't have to give it to me right now," I said.

"Here," he said. In a glance I saw that he was holding out all of it, fifties and twenties, the whole stack that Billy had paid him for the Fender. I was stunned. I kept looking from the road to the money.

"Daniel..."

"You look after it," he said with a good-natured shrug.

I was ashamed. I'd tried to threaten it out of him, sneak it away from him. Now he was offering it to me all on his own.

"Okay," I said and cleared my throat, because there was a catch in it.

Before I took the money, Daniel peeled off one twenty-dollar bill.

"For Easton," he said, grinning.

TWELVE

It was barely nine o'clock and the Times Change Cafe wasn't open yet, so I drove back to the Petro-Canada. The coffee was fresh and I took a deep gulp, not caring if I scalded my mouth. Daniel was just about to put money into the Coke machine but looking at me, he changed his mind and got a coffee, too. I watched him ladle sugar into it and shook my head. I couldn't understand why he wasn't hung over.

I asked the guy behind the counter if there was some place we could get a shower.

"Sure," he said. "The Holiday Inn in Winnipeg."

We wound up washing in the men's room, shoulder to shoulder. It was pretty clean, but small; there was only one sink. We discovered we both shaved exactly the same way — stroke for stroke. Dad's way. It made us laugh. I filled up more of the mirror, but aside from that we could have been shaving twins. It had been a long time since we'd shared a bathroom.

"This girl from Easton," I said, dunking my razor. "How'd you ever meet her?"

"At SunJam," Daniel said. "She's a singer, mostly alt — alternative, Shady Roy and like that — but she could do blues. She's got that smoky voice. I think she can hit notes lower than me. She took third place in the vocalist category but she should have gotten first. She's fantastic. I tell her that all the time," he finished softly.

I was intrigued. "How? I mean, do you phone each other?"

"We write. Sometimes she sends me lyrics. If I can work up music for them, I'll put it on cassette for her. She says she loves my music. I sent her the tape of Blue Prairie before anyone else."

I thought of my own first girlfriends, the awkward weeks of not knowing what to say, grateful to get to the necking part because that at least you knew how to do. Daniel writing songs for this girl with the smoky voice seemed...serious.

"Does Mom know?" I said suddenly.

"No! Well, maybe. She sees I get letters. But I don't tell her anything."

I knew what he meant. He loved Mom and Dad, but they were still parents.

As soon as we were finished, we pulled on clean shirts and gathered up our stuff. But with my hand on the doorknob, I turned back to him.

"What's her name?"

He hesitated. The color showed up bright on his smooth face.

"Never mind," I said, pushing out.

"Chantel." The word seemed to slip over my shoulder, so soft it was almost lost in the whisper of the door. The revelation spread through me. I wasn't the only one he'd been singing for last night. I couldn't remember anything about the song, except that it was nice. It made me wish I'd listened better.

Outside at the truck, Daniel announced he was hungry. Momentous news. I rummaged through our food supplies until I found a box of cereal. It was one of my all-time favorites, the kind that claims to be low sugar but tastes like candy anyway. I could eat this stuff all day, bowl not required.

Daniel looked at me blankly. "Well, I can't have it without milk."

I sighed. I went back into the station and came out with a carton of milk. I drank half of it in two long swallows. Then I pulled apart the spout until it was an open square, and poured the cereal inside.

"Look for a long spoon," I said.

Daniel grinned.

We were supposed to call home every day. This seemed like the right time. I had all the money in my pocket and Daniel was eating something, before noon.

"You're spoiled, you know," I said lightly as I punched in the phone number. "Mom never bought that kind when I was at home."

"That's because you'd go through it in an hour," Daniel said.

"Oh, get real."

"You would! Right after school. I've seen you."

Mom picked up the phone before the second ring. She must have been sitting on it. The questions came out rapid-fire from the Health and Safety Department: How were we? Where were we? Did we wake up freezing?

"Yeah, Mom, we woke up dead," I teased. She didn't think it was funny.

"I mean it, Jens. You listen to the weather reports. If it even threatens to go below zero, you guys get into a motel. It doesn't have to be a nice place. And whatever you do, don't get drunk."

I felt a guilty tug. "Okay. Sure. How come?"

"Alcohol lowers sensation. You can't feel how cold you are. Hypothermia sets in and you don't even know it." There was a pause. "How's Daniel?"

"Fine. He's eating breakfast. Want to say hi?" I was uncomfortable with a conversation that had both alcohol and Daniel in it.

"Sure. But after that, your father wants to talk to you."

There was something in the way she said it, an odd tone that pulled my insides tight. I handed the phone to Daniel, my mind running.

Everything's still okay, I told myself. Sy told you to keep the truck until Monday and it's only Sunday. You're calling in tomorrow. You're still okay.

"Pas mal. Mais, il est assez moody, comme toujours..."

I gave Daniel a little shove on the back. "Stop it. I hate that."

He turned, startled.

"And hurry up. I'm supposed to talk to Dad."

He grimaced at me, but finally I took the phone again.

"Hi, Dad."

"How are you?" It had only been a day, but the deep rumble of his voice was like a hand on my shoulder.

"We're good. Tell Mom to stop worrying."

"You're sure you have enough money, in case of emergency?" he said.

I told him we were fine. Everything was fine.

"Your landlord called," he said.

My stomach dropped, a dizzying pitch as my life boomeranged back at me. I'd forgotten about Mr. Delbeggio. In the wake of everything else – my job and the truck and Daniel – that mess had been swept aside. Suddenly I was standing in it again, up to my ass in it, naked. And my father knew. My heart began to run.

"You know, I think...I think there's been a misunderstanding," I said quickly. "I left him the key and maybe he thinks...maybe he doesn't know I'm on holidays. I'll call him. I can clear this up. I'll call him first thing tomorrow."

"Jens," Dad said, "is there something you want to talk to me about?"

For a moment I couldn't speak. My body was stretched, fingers curled over the top of the phone cubicle as if I was hanging there, suspended.

But I couldn't let go, not yet. I had to do this thing for Daniel and I could make it work – I was making it! – if I had more time. I just needed more time.

"No, it's okay. Really." I could barely breathe. "Everything's okay. I'll call him tomorrow. And

I'll talk to you and Mom...soon. Don't worry." I hung up.

"What'd he want? Did you tell him we were going to Easton?" Daniel said through a mouthful, behind me.

The sound of his eager, earnest crunching was suddenly unbearable.

"Get in the truck. We're leaving now," I said without turning around.

"It's okay for Mom to know, but I don't want Dad..."

"Just get in the goddamn truck!"

Daniel shut up. I heard him pitch the milk container into the garbage, a solid thunk against the metal as he passed it.

I got the box of cereal out of the back and put it on the seat beside me while I drove. Inside an hour I had emptied it, one handful at a time.

A lot of people speed on the prairie. It's not just that you can – the endless asphalt spread out like a runway, flat and straight and open. The problem is everything else – fields so huge you can see the curve of the earth, the sky over you like an enormous blue bowl. You lose track of how big you are, how fast you're going.

My old gym teacher, Mr. Flett, had come from Ontario, where highways are lined with trees and industrial parks, and you never lose sight of the bumper ahead of yours. He said it bothered him to drive in Manitoba.

"You feel like this little...speck," he laughed. "You feel like you're falling."

For me, that Sunday, I couldn't fall fast enough. Every now and then Daniel would glance at the speedometer.

"Jesus, Jens! You're going to get a ticket."

"When you get your license, you can have an opinion."

I think he was nervous. Now that we were actually on our way to Easton, he wasn't in such a hurry to get there. I'd asked him if he wanted to phone Chantel ahead.

"No! I don't want to make a big deal out of this. I want it to be like we're just passing through."

"We are just passing through," I warned him. "If there's nowhere to do a gig, we won't stay long."

But I let him play the radio to feel better; I even let him choose the station. There was nothing near blues so he picked heavy metal. The deep, rhythmic blare of electric guitar blocked out any chance of conversation, and I think we were both grateful. Daniel stared out the window, fingers drumming perfect time on his thigh.

I was doing mental math. I'd decided that since I'd beaten my goal last night by seventy-five percent, I could do it again. Only I had to beat what I'd hit yesterday — thirty-five plus seventy-five percent made sixty-one tapes the magic number. I felt a rush of adrenaline and fear. It was outrageous — impossible. But today was Sunday and tomorrow was Monday, and now I had two phone calls I didn't know how I was going to make. The lure of sixty-one tapes kept my eyes on the road and my foot on the gas.

Easton was a surprise. Not just a cluster of buildings along the highway, it was a real town set off to the south, bigger even than Rosetown. The noon sun had burned off the white cover of clouds and the day seemed bright and hopeful. I drove up and down the streets, taking stock: three schools, four churches, a few strip malls, banks, a brand new recreational center. There was even a little block of apartments, three stories high, and what seemed to be a medical center or small hospital. When we passed the Golden Arches, I knew we'd hit a metropolis.

"This place has possibilities," I told Daniel excitedly. "If not for today, then tomorrow. But I want to get on it. Do you think Chantel could give us some ideas? After all, this is her town. Where does she live?"

It was too much, too fast. Daniel looked panicked. "Wait, maybe...maybe I should phone first..."

I pulled up to a convenience store, with phones along the outside wall, and handed him a quarter.

"Remember packaging," I said. "Put a flag on your aerial."

He turned away quickly. I realized Chantel was not someone to joke about and I resolved to shut up. Daniel took things hard, harder than me. And this was probably the first girl who mattered.

I watched him walk away, trying to remember what that was like. Before you knew that it was just war games. Before you knew it was all of her friends against all of yours, and that it was your Rosetown Raiders jersey that was the prize, and it didn't matter that you were in it. Yet all around you the world was shouting, "Hey, what do you care? You're getting laid!"

I had never written songs for anybody. I bit my lip and looked out my side window, so Daniel wouldn't think I was staring at him.

It seemed to take a long time. Finally he walked back to the driver's side. I unrolled the window.

"She wasn't home so I tried her at work," Daniel said. "She has a break in about twenty minutes." He grinned, a little shell-shocked, as if he didn't believe it. "She...she said yeah. Come over. Right now."

"And you! You were worried." I reached through the window and pushed his head, mussing his hair. His smile never dipped. "So get in. I'll take you over."

"Jens, I'm just going to walk." He glanced behind him. "I'm pretty sure I know where it is. I just want to do this alone." He was already backing away. "I'll meet you here in an hour, I promise."

He swung around abruptly before I could answer, and set off in a determined stride. I was fiercely disappointed. I couldn't even see her? My brother's first girlfriend, three hundred kilometers of buildup, and I couldn't even see what she looked like?

As Daniel rounded the corner at the end of the block, out of sight, my heart started to run lightly. I got out and locked the door.

Jens, this isn't nice, I told myself. But curiosity was pulling me on in sharp, quick tugs. This was another part of my brother I didn't know. What kind of girl would he go for? What kind of girl would go for him? I had to see this Chantel with the smoky voice.

I followed him easily from two blocks back. He never looked behind him, he was so intent on where he was going. When he turned from the business part of town into residential, tree-lined streets, it made me wonder. Was she babysitting or working in somebody's home? Another turn took us clear, past a school, heading toward the building with the big green cross.

It was nerve-wracking inside the hospital, close quarters and sudden turns. I was caught between the fear of being seen and losing him completely. Luckily the hallways were busy, patients and staff in a moving stream of white and pastels. His blue jean jacket was easy to follow.

I was wondering what kind of job a teenaged girl could get in a hospital but Daniel stopped in front of the small cafeteria. At the end of the hall, I ducked back. I just want to see her, I promised. And then I'll go.

When I allowed myself to peek around the corner he was still there, hands in his pockets, a dark denim figure against the pale green wall. He looked older than when he was standing next to me.

And then she saw him, too. She broke out of the swift-moving ranks into a little jog and caught him around the shoulders in an excited squeeze. She was as tall as he was, or taller. Her hair was tied back in a French braid, dark blond painted with streaks of yellow white. But I was looking at her clothes, the pink top and pants that pushed out in curvy breasts and hips. It was a uniform.

Even at this distance I could see the light in Daniel's face. She said something that made him laugh, and he walked into the cafeteria with her, still beaming. I leaned against the wall.

Chantel wasn't a girl, she was a woman. She was older than me, I was sure of it. Daniel was sixteen – a kid. He'd probably argue with me but I'd been sixteen and I knew. Women, beautiful women, didn't get involved with kids. He was lining up for a broken heart.

And Chantel wasn't steering him away. I saw it again, the press of her tall, curvy body against him. That was not a friendly hug. That was not about lyrics. My face flamed. What was this lady's head game?

I had made a promise in the parking lot, to keep my mouth shut, to stay back. But the rules had changed – this woman had changed them. Whatever she was up to, I was going to find out. Daniel was my little brother.

I strode into the cafeteria.

THIRTEEN

Daniel and Chantel were by the wall, at a table for four. They didn't notice me until I was standing right beside them.

Chantel looked up. Her eyes were too green – probably tinted contacts. She had a row of hoops and studs decorating the curve of one ear, and a gold ring through the ridge of the opposite eyebrow. Like her hair, they were bleached. Because I was standing I couldn't help but see down past the collar of her shirt to the edge of white lace that strained over a breast, barely hiding a pink and red tattoo.

"Hi, how are you today?" I said, offering my hand to her. She took it, but looked quizzically across the table at Daniel.

"I can see that you've chosen one of our most popular models," I said, gesturing at my brother but not looking at him. "Many women... ladies...like the sports coupe because it's so responsive, easy to handle. Zero to sixty in under twelve seconds. Do you plan to take it on the highway?"

Chantel laughed, a single breath.

"This is a joke, right?" she said to Daniel.

"Oh, yeah. A big fucking joke."

Murder was in his voice, but I knew my brother. He wouldn't blow up in public.

"I'm Jens..." I said.

"I know. The used car guy."

"New," I corrected. "The new car and truck guy." It sounded shabby even coming from me. I dropped into the chair beside Daniel.

"Don't sit down, Jens. What are you doing here? What do you want?!"

"Just relax, okay?" I told him. "I thought you might forget to ask Chantel about where we could get a gig tonight."

"He didn't get much of a chance," Chantel said. She was watching me, one corner of her mouth crimped, not quite a smile. "But since you asked, I'll tell you, it's a tight little town. Smiley's used to book singles, doubles, even the occasional three-piece, but now it's a sports bar. They're allowed to shoot you if you get in front of the TV. The Highland Hotel has a lounge and they even had a stage, a platform big enough for a drum kit — but that's where they put in the VLTs."

She did have a smoky voice. Not masculine, not really deep, but the sound seemed to come from her chest, like someone on the very last day of a cold. It made you listen.

"There's a dessert place that lets singers and musicians get up on Thursday nights, but it's kind of a free-for-all jam session," Chantel continued.

"We can't wait until Thursday night," I said.

"And then there's the Heartland Arena."

I perked up. "The rec center? That'd be great! How do we get in there?"

Now Chantel did smile. "Well, musicians don't actually get *inside*..."

"Forget it. We're not busking."

"I'd love it," Daniel blurted.

He was twisted in his seat, leaning against the wall, eyes like nails as he stared at me.

"That's not what you want," I said.

"Yeah, it is," he answered defiantly. "I want to open my case and just play for whoever walks by. Maybe there'll be a bunch of us. We'll compete for loose change."

My collar chafed my neck.

"I think there's a curling bonspiel or something on tonight. Lots of people," Chantel said, green eyes twinkling. "Can I come, too?"

Daniel leaned suddenly across the table. "Yeah! Would you? Do you want to sing? I can play whatever you want."

I winced. Jesus, Daniel. Stick your heart back in your shirt.

Chantel smiled and put her hand on top of his two that were earnestly clenched on the tabletop. "I don't know. It's your gig."

"We...we've got to do Starlight," Daniel said, flustered, but he didn't move his hands away. "What'd you think of that little riff I put into the chorus?"

"It's so edgy. I loved it."

"I have to hear you sing that," Daniel insisted.

"It's got balls, doesn't it? But I renamed it to 'I See Stars.'" Chantel's voice dropped and she started to sing softly. *"I see stars when you give it to me, stars when you kiss me, stars make me come ... out at night..."*

I straightened up in my chair, face prickling. Edgy wasn't the word for it.

"Look, I hate to rain on your parade, but we've got an agenda. We're out here to sell tapes, get some exposure." I didn't know what Daniel had told her about Mogen Kruse. I hoped nothing. "We don't have time for street shows."

Daniel still had one hand on the table, his

long, knobby fingers interlocked with Chantel's. He didn't take his eyes off her.

"You're the salesman, Jens," he said. "If we have to sell tapes, you figure out how. That's your job. But we're doing this tonight."

Chantel was watching me boldly. "Nice to finally meet you, Jens," she said. "I never met a new car and truck guy before."

I stood. "Yeah, you, too. Daniel, I'll catch up with you at the truck."

I walked away, feeling her laughter against my back, although I never heard it.

The day outside was still bright and sunny, but it didn't help. I wasn't sure who I was madder at — them or me. Busking! I knew Daniel was doing it to bug me, but I couldn't imagine why Chantel would want to join him, except for the same reason. I wondered what he'd told her about me.

I'd really screwed this up. I'd gone in to figure her out and come away with nothing, except that Daniel melted like butter around her. Maybe that was it. She liked the power over him. Or maybe it was the music thing. She wanted him to keep pumping out songs for her lyrics.

I see stars when you give it to me, stars when you kiss me...

The memory surged through my body, a

warm rush that I couldn't stop. I kept walking but I slowed. She's out of your league, Daniel, I thought.

But I didn't know what to do about it.

Back at the truck I realized I was hungry. With the cereal gone I knew that all the non-cook items left were chips and crackers. I didn't want crackers. Daniel was out there having a good time, spending the Fender money. Well, so could I.

The dessert place served sandwiches, too. I ordered a clubhouse at the counter and stood there waiting for it. It seemed to me the restaurant was full of couples, chairs pulled in close together. I didn't want to sit by myself.

The cashier came back. "I forgot to ask. Is that to stay or to go?"

"To go, I guess."

She marked it on the bill. "Too bad," she murmured as she turned away.

I looked after her, the swing of her hips, the saucy bounce of her dark, shoulder-length hair. Another Marcy. Waitresses seemed to like me, and I found it easy to kid around with them, maybe because I knew I could pay the bill and go. It wasn't like meeting someone.

I ate in the truck, trying to figure out how I was going to move sixty-one tapes. Easton was a big town — five thousand plus. A curling bonspiel would draw hundreds of people, but I didn't know if they were Daniel's kind of audience. And what if there were other musicians? They only asked for loose change. I wanted an eight-dollar commitment. We weren't going to beat those guys on price.

After an hour, I gave up thinking about it. What was taking Daniel? Chantel couldn't still be on her break. I drove around Easton, past the music store and McDonald's, anywhere he might be. I thought about going back to the hospital to ask for Chantel, then realized I didn't know her last name or even what department she worked in. I parked at the convenience store again.

He's probably just pissed off at you, I told myself. He's sixteen years old and Easton isn't New York. Yet I could feel my stomach knotting. Don't lose him, Mom had said.

I hung on for another forty-five minutes. Then I drove up and down every street, more carefully this time, checking all the shadows and alleys. When I slowly circled the school playgrounds, mothers sat up on their benches, alert. But I was worried, too.

Where the hell could he be? Why would he do this? Even if you're mad at someone you don't...scare them.

I parked at the hospital. It was a long shot

but I was desperate. I didn't know what I'd do if he wasn't there.

I was hurrying up to the front door when I saw the familiar shape of denim and dark hair in the distance, across the big asphalt drive and a park. He was leaving Easton's one apartment building. I almost sagged with relief.

"Daniel!" I called.

He kept walking. I broke into a run after him.

"Daniel!"

I was close enough but still he wouldn't turn around. Barreling over the field, running like I hadn't in a long time, I wanted to scream it in his ear.

I caught him by the shoulders, a frustrated tackle that sent us both crashing onto somebody's lawn. I came down on him harder than I meant to, felt the sickening crunch, but I couldn't stop the momentum. Before I could move to get up, his elbow came back at me.

Sharp pain between my ribs sucked my breath away and I couldn't get it back. Daniel shoved me off, then lunged after me, straddled me, pounding with the sides of his clenched fists. It was all I could do to get my arms up over my face.

Blow after solid blow made my head spin. He was stronger than I ever expected, and I still couldn't breathe. The feeling came up from the pit of my stomach, a gust of adrenaline or raw fear — I thought I was going to suffocate.

I threw him off in a wild thrust, sent him tumbling onto the sidewalk. I managed to roll over onto my hands and knees, crouched like a sick animal. I drew in shallow, creaking breaths, staring hard at the grass to blot out the pain.

"Are you trying to kill me?!" Daniel cried.

I couldn't speak yet. Breathe, Jens.

Daniel sat back on his haunches, shaken. "I mean, you jump me from behind...scare the shit out of me, I don't know what..." He seemed to notice my condition for the first time and leaned closer. "Jens, are you okay? Say something."

"Are...you...deaf?!" I gasped.

I straightened at last, the world still blurred around the edges. When I moved to stand, he held out his arm but I ignored it. I could get up on my own. We started down the street, back the way I'd come. I wasn't moving fast.

"Where the hell have you been?" I said.

He nodded toward the apartment block. "At Chantel's. She gave me a key. She asked if I would change the strings on her guitar and tune it."

"For two hours?! Didn't you think of me sitting there? Didn't you think I'd be worried?"

He looked away. I saw a red scrape on his

cheekbone, where he'd rubbed the pavement.

"Why? You didn't think of me sitting there," he said finally. "All I wanted was twenty minutes, just her and me. But you have to follow me like I'm an idiot you can't let out of your sight, Daniel, the retard..."

"Oh, come on —"

"Then you shove your way in with some stupid line," he continued, a quiver in his voice. "Stand there grinning. You can get anybody but you wouldn't let me have twenty minutes!"

He didn't understand. "Daniel...how old is she?"

"I don't know and I don't care."

"Well, you should care —"

He turned on me, his eyes like dark liquid. "You know what, Jens? Most people bore me. And I bore them. Oh, yeah, I'm the guy with the guitar. That's good for about two minutes. I sit in school feeling like a goddamn... fencepost. All the crap they're shoveling at me, I understand it just fine, but I can't care about it. I think, if I have to live in this, I'm going to die."

I thought of him calling Kruse four times a day. Jack Lahanni would say Daniel had drive, too.

"Jim Renders' house. Is that where you go?" I said.

He looked shocked that I knew. But the

Renders had two working parents and five rowdy sons. Kids had been going there to drink for a decade.

We were walking again. "So you need a boost to get through the afternoon, too?"

"Not every afternoon..."

"You're breaking Mom's heart," I said.

"Well, what about my heart?" Daniel shot back. Then his voice dropped. "Chantel is the most exciting person I know. She's interesting. And we care about the same things. Sure, we have different styles, but it's the same *stuff*. And I think she likes me," he finished softly.

Or does she like what you give her? I didn't say it. I was thinking of the way he'd lunged at me, pounded on me, even after he knew who it was.

We had reached the truck. The sun was still high in the sky but I knew it was late afternoon. A wasted day.

"You know, we'd better find a place to camp," I started.

"Chantel said we could stay overnight at her place."

"She lives alone?" I asked cautiously.

"Yeah. She said we could sleep on the floor. Just bring our sleeping bags up."

The idea tugged me in different directions. I didn't trust this woman who'd hold hands with a sixteen-year-old in public, who sang like she was pressed up against you, moaning into your ear. I didn't know what I might say to her before the night was out.

But to sleep inside, even on the floor. To have a shower...I was feeling dirtier by the minute.

"We'll see," I said. We drove over to the apartment and I followed Daniel up to the third floor. He pulled out the key almost proudly, but the door swung open before he could get it in the lock. She was already home.

"Men," she said cheerfully. "I can hear you tromping around a mile away."

She had changed out of her uniform. Tight black jeans and tank top, cut so low I imagined I could see the pink edge of her tattoo every time she moved. Her hair was undone and it fell just past her shoulders, rippled from the braid, white-blonde strands tangled in with gold and brown. She was smoking a cigarette.

"And you work in a hospital," I said as I walked in.

"Yeah, but I didn't take an oath. Hey, what happened?" she said, reaching to touch Daniel's cheek.

He drew back, a little embarrassed. "We were just —"

"Wrestling," I said.

She looked me up and down. "Oh, and I bet *that* was fair."

I let go a short breath. I'd probably have a bruise the size of a baseball between my ribs — the spot still throbbed. It might have been a lucky shot but Daniel had nailed me worse than I'd hurt him.

He was already on the couch, hoisting Chantel's acoustic over his knee. "What'd you think? Did you take it for a spin?" He struck a few chords, as pleased as if he'd built the thing.

Chantel laughed. "Well, I don't come home from work and run to the guitar..."

"Why not?"

She laughed again and dropped onto the couch beside him. "Hey, I was wondering if you'd show me something. I think I'm doing this wrong..."

She took the guitar from him and strummed through a section of a song — his or one of hers, I couldn't tell. To be honest, it was a shock, the halting gaps as she fumbled over the frets, the sudden jangle of an off note. When Daniel played, the sound seemed to flow out of him, like breathing. His big-knuckled hands and knobby fingers looked awkward holding a pencil or a hammer, but they flew over those strings like he owned them.

Chantel finished and looked up at him, biting her lip. He was smiling at her.

"Okay," my brother said patiently. "That's pretty good. Let's start with the bar chords..."

They might as well have been speaking French. I drifted around the living room, touching things.

It was as small as my own had been, or smaller, but bright with strangeness: a quirky orange lawn chair; a cat clock with moving eyes. There was a fully inflated punching clown — Boffo — and big aluminum wind chimes hanging from the ceiling. There were no family pictures, but one of a band she must have been in.

It was a promotional photo. Chantel up front in black leather and bright pink lipstick, four snarky rock and roll clones behind her — skinny, sullen guys you'd mow down like grass on a football field. I stood looking at those pink lips and the ring that glinted through her eyebrow, gold against gold. I wondered how many of the band had made her see stars.

Behind me, the lesson was over and rehearsal had started, sort of. Daniel had a firm grip on the guitar again and he was playing whatever she wanted. Chantel's smoky voice seemed to take over the small room but it was obvious they'd never played together. There were lots of screw-ups and stumbles that made them laugh like kids.

My hands were clasped behind my back. Today was Sunday and tomorrow was Monday, and I had sixty-one tapes to sell.

"What time does this curling thing get going?" I broke in. "Maybe you should practice, Daniel. Or get cleaned up."

There was a half-second of silence.

"You want something to do, Jens?" Chantel said. "Make supper, if you can."

FOURTEEN

"I can cook," I said. "I'm a great cook. Fantastic. What do you want? I can make anything."

Chantel had nothing defrosted. "Get creative," she shrugged. "Look around. That's the mark of a master anyway."

"Okay, I will." I tossed my jacket and pushed up my sleeves. All the dirty dishes on the counter I just cleared into the sink, not minding the noise. She'd see. They weren't the only artists in the place.

I'd started cooking at home when Dad was in the hospital. So many nights Mom stayed with him late, and I'd make supper for Daniel and me. Once we got tired of grilled cheese sandwiches, I started to experiment. I could get completely absorbed chopping and frying, looking for new things to throw into the pan. It surprised me that it was fun. It surprised everyone else that I was good at it. When Dad came home and Mom went to work, I still cooked a couple of nights a week. I liked the feeling that I was helping.

I rummaged in Chantel's fridge for eggs — jackpot. You can do a hundred things with eggs. Finding the green pepper, mushrooms and cheese was pure bonus; it made the decision for me. Any chimp can scramble or fry, but a good omelet, that's a test of skill.

I found a non-stick skillet in the cupboard and twirled it once by the handle before I set it on the element. Daniel and Chantel were back at it, bursts of music and chatter, but it didn't bother me now. I had a mission.

The secret to my omelets is that I fry the ingredients separately and don't overcook the eggs. And I don't just pour the batter into the pan and hope for the best. Every now and then I scrape up through the center with the flipper, lifting the pan at a forty-five degree angle so what's liquid runs into the gap, spreading the egg thinner, cooking it more evenly. I caught Chantel watching me while I held the pan in the air.

My other secret is Tabasco sauce — just a few squirts — in the egg mixture. You don't ask whether anybody wants it, you just do it.

The first two omelets were good but the third was perfect. Magazine quality, with extra cheese melted over the top, for effect. I made sure she got that one. There was no table so we ate in the living room, plates on our knees, sharing toast from one platter. I'd run out of clean dishes.

Chantel was impressed, especially when she tasted it.

"I don't believe it," she said. "An eighteen-year-old who can cook."

"Nineteen," I said. "I'm almost nineteen."

She didn't seem to hear, but looked from Daniel to me. "A songwriter and a chef. If you were one man I'd marry you."

It was getting late. The bonspiel started at eight so I thought we should be set up by seven. I was getting nervous and a little revved, in spite of myself. I hated the whole busking thing but maybe there was an opportunity here that I just didn't know about.

I sent Daniel in for a shower first. "And hurry up. I want one, too," I said.

Chantel was leaning back on the couch, smoking a cigarette, her nipples outlined under her T-shirt. I put myself in the kitchen and started to clean up.

"Daniel never told me what you did at the hospital," I said, scrubbing out the skillet. "Nursing?"

"Blood lab. I'm a technician."

"You must have been a biology major. Which university?"

"U of M."

"Medical is pretty tough," I called over the running water. "Was it a long program? Three, four years...?"

"Twenty-two." Her voice was suddenly close. I turned to see her leaning in the doorway to the kitchen.

"What?"

"I'm twenty-two," she said. "That's what you're trying to find out, isn't it?"

I turned off the tap.

"My brother is sixteen," I said.

"I know. I sent him a card. Did you?"

I hadn't, and she knew it. She seemed to know a lot about me, the new car and truck guy. I didn't like it.

"What do you want from him? What are you after?" I asked bluntly.

She took a drag of her cigarette, pink lips around the white filter. "I don't think I owe you an explanation," she said.

"No, but you might owe my mom."

I'd hit a nerve. She turned away and wandered back into the living room, arms folded over her chest. I followed, grabbing a dish towel for my wet hands.

"You can't play games with him. That's not fair. He's a kid," I said.

"He's brilliant." She turned around. "I don't think you appreciate that. Maybe he's just your little brother but people are starting to notice him."

There was a copy of Blue Prairie on the end table and she scooped it up. "Producers don't foot the bill for demo tapes, Jens, not unless they think they're going to make a whole lot of money on you later. What Daniel got would cost the average peon like me two, even three grand."

I felt struck. Kruse said we owed him *five*.

Chantel continued on. "The world is full of great guitarists, but he's *writing* those songs. At sixteen. That's exciting."

My mind was trying to move in two gears at once. "You're saying it's three grand for a demo and about five hundred tapes?"

She nodded toward the promo picture on the wall. "That's the top end. We priced out five places. Right before we split up," she finished quietly.

No wonder Kruse had blown up when I asked what the tapes were worth – he was over-charging Daniel. But I wasn't about to tell our troubles to Chantel.

"So Daniel's talented," I said. "That excites you."

She met me dead on with her clear green eyes. "I like him. He's sweet. He doesn't use people." She stubbed out her cigarette in an ashtray, pressing it down twice, three times. "And he's lonely. Who couldn't understand that?"

The soft sound of her voice surprised me. I didn't think women like Chantel were ever without...company. But then Daniel thought I could get anybody I wanted, too.

He walked in, combing his damp hair.

"I left you a towel," he said.

"Thanks, here's one for you," I said, draping the wet dish towel against his neck as I hurried by. He grabbed it off and snapped it at me, but he hit the closed door. Way too slow.

I stripped off my clothes, my mind running back to Mogen Kruse. That rip-off artist! He'd built the cost of the "free" recording session into the price, and then some. His offer to represent Daniel was so Mom and Dad wouldn't look anywhere else. But a contract was a contract. Overcharging might be wrong but it wasn't illegal.

And yet I couldn't stop the rush of sudden hope. Now that I knew what was fair I might have a lever, a bargaining chip to beat down the amount we owed him. If I showed up with two and a half thousand dollars, he'd probably take it. But I wouldn't tell Daniel yet; I didn't want him to slow down.

It felt good to get under the hot water and scrub the last two days away. Maybe it felt too good. The memory of pink lips and hard nipples rubbed against me as I soaped up with care. A lot of care. Daniel wasn't the only one who knew about lonely.

You have sixty-one tapes to sell, I told myself finally. Stay hungry.

I eased the temperature from warm to cool, then finally cold.

The counter around the sink was crowded with make-up, brushes and perfume. A flowery female scent rose up with the steam. I rubbed a circle on the mirror so I could comb my hair. It was running lighter than usual, from all the sunny days. Brown eyes, blunt jaw. Shoulders that filled up the mirror. You're not so bad, I told myself.

I walked out into the living room. Daniel and Chantel were leaning against the wall, wrapped up together, deep in each other's mouths. She had one hand clenched in the back of his hair, the other at his waist, under his shirt.

"We'd better go," I said. My voice sounded raw. I hit Boffo the clown on my way out.

We arrived at the rec center just before seven. I stopped the truck across the street and got out for a look. It was still daylight, evening sun that gave everything a bronze tint and long shadows. There were already cars in the parking lot and clusters of people standing around socializing. Most surrounded the three or four trucks that had their tailgates open; that's where the beer flowed from. I was amazed. I'd seen tailgate parties for football, but curling? It must be the biggest sport in town.

There was a long wall between the parking lot and the main entrance, and that's where the musicians were set up – already two guitar players and one saxophone. I could understand their reasoning: Everyone would have to pass by them to get inside. But no one was making that walk yet. The musicians had their cases open, playing to the open air, one circle of music bleeding into the next.

Daniel was watching them eagerly.

"Do you know anyone?" he asked Chantel.

"That's Andy Larson at the end," she said.

"Let's go talk to him. Jens, let me open the back."

"Wait." I put a hand on his shoulder, holding him. If I let Daniel join the wall he'd be lost. I had to do something that would make him stand out, show that he was above the others. We were out here to sell tapes.

A burst of laughter made me look over at the

parking lot again. That's where the party was. I had a brainstorm.

"If only we had an extension cord," I said.

My brother looked at me. "Of course we do. It's in that bag with my extra strings and picks and stuff. Why?"

My arm flew around his neck, tugging him into a headlock. "Daniel, you're brilliant!" I buzzed the top of his head with my knuckles.

He wriggled out of my grip and looked at me suspiciously, dark hair standing up. "Why? What are we going to do?"

But I wouldn't tell him yet. I drove into the parking lot, past the party people, to the corner of the lot marked "Staff," and backed into a stall.

Manitoba winters are brutal. You can't let a car sit all day at minus twenty – or thirty – and expect it to start. Most businesses have a rack of electrical outlets for their employees to plug in. My only fear was that the rec center had switched off the breaker because it was spring.

Daniel watched me unload his guitar and the amps.

"Are you nuts?! Jens, you don't busk with an electric."

"Then think of it as an open-air concert."

He gestured at the musicians along the wall. "I'll drown them out. They'll hate me!"

Chantel was grinning, leaning against the

truck. She had on a little black leather jacket, tight and short. I was sure she couldn't zip it up all the way. "So let them hate you. You're leaving tomorrow anyway. I think it takes balls."

The compliment made him blush, but he took an uncertain step toward her.

"I thought you and me were going to sing together. We can't sing electric without a mike."

"Later," I cut in. "Once we have a crowd and they know you're here. Why don't you get the acoustic out right now? And grab some tapes, too."

As soon as he left, I closed in on Chantel.

"Listen, thanks. But I need more help. I want him to get up on the hood."

She laughed out loud, a single gust of disbelief. "You never quit, do you?"

I smiled back at her. "If I was ice cream, I'd be Tiger-Tiger."

I let Daniel set up and start tuning in front of the truck. To my relief the cords reached and the power was still on. I stacked the guitar cases on top of each other and began building a display of cassettes.

"Why don't you put those up here," Daniel said, touching the hood. "People could see them better."

I looked at Chantel.

"That's where you're going to be," she said.

"What?!"

My instincts had been right. My brother was a tough sell. Finally I tugged him aside.

"Daniel, to get people over here, you've got to do something, be different. We don't have a lot of time. If you think you're good, you've got to be willing to stand up and prove it."

"But not on the truck!"

"Why not?"

He looked away. "It's stupid. It's like...showing off."

"Yeah, it is! And if you're good enough, you've got that right."

"I'll be embarrassed."

"So wear the hat," I said. Now he was embarrassed, that I knew what it was for. I hurried on. "And you said you didn't care what people thought, anyway."

"It's easy for you to talk! You don't have to get up there."

"No, but I will," I said. "I'll introduce you."

His face was so full of disbelief it was almost a taunt. "You'll stand up on this truck and say, Here's Daniel Desroschers and he's great?"

The name stuck in my throat like a claw. It would choke me.

"I'll shout it," I promised.

"And you'll charge ten bucks a tape?"

"I...will."

He was grinning now. "And every morning you'll get down on your knees and kiss my —"

I grabbed for another headlock, a good one this time, but he was half expecting it and put up a decent struggle. Chantel looked over in alarm, thinking it was a fight, until she heard him laugh.

I did everything I could think of to sell tapes. Heart thumping, I stood on my truck hood in front of him and announced to the nearly full parking lot that they were about to hear the best new guitarist in the province of Manitoba. I leapt to the ground and Daniel burst into "Night Drive," the instrumental killer he'd opened at the Starling Legion with.

I was close enough to know he was shaking. The hat hid his face; his head was so low his chin almost touched his chest, as he pretended to watch his fingering. Yet it looked strangely cool, as if he didn't care.

The sight and the sound of him — that driving, electric dead run of a song — pulled people in. I could see the question in their faces. Who the hell was this kid on the truck? I was there with the answer, shaking hands and showing the tape.

"Where do we throw the money?" a woman asked.

I politely explained my brother was a professional and that he would be glad to autograph a cassette for her, at his next break.

"How much?" she said, picking one up.

I took a nervous breath. But I'd promised him. "Nine ninety-five."

She seemed to study it for a long time. "Can you change a twenty?"

I could have kissed her.

At first Chantel was stationed in the crowd to applaud, get people going. When I realized we didn't need it, I asked her to take an armful of tapes over to the party trucks.

"Oh, right! Should I wear bunny ears and a poofy little tail, too?"

Her hands were on her hips, black denim stretched tight. I swallowed. "You...you'd knock them over in a paper bag."

The compliment caught her off guard. "Salesmen!" she said finally, shaking her head, yet I could have sworn she was blushing. She loaded up on tapes, and sold six. I think she was surprised that it worked.

I'd planned to coach Daniel on what songs to play, except I got busy talking to people and taking money. A pack of twelve- and thirteen-year-old girls cornered me against the side of the truck, peppering me with questions about Daniel. How old was he? Where did he live? Did he have a girlfriend?

"No," I said.

That sold three tapes. Their whole group stood around, giggling and whispering as they waited for the autographs.

I didn't have to worry about my brother. He'd learned something in Starling. If the crowd started to thin, he'd pick up on a song everybody knew, drawing over the people just getting out of their cars. It amazed me again. He *could* play anyone, from Hendrix to Henley, and every song Colin James had ever written or touched.

At 7:30 he took a break, looking relieved as he slid down onto the ground. He was immediately surrounded by people who wanted their tapes signed. I was worried because I hadn't warned him about it, yet he slung off the guitar and handed it to me like I was a roadie. I watched the smooth flow of movements — how he deftly unwrapped the plastic, opened the case and signed the paper sleeve with a flourish — and realized he'd practiced this. It reminded me of when I'd got my business cards, standing in front of the mirror, perfecting the smile as I held one out, the slightest tilt of a bow.

I couldn't resist. I nudged my way in next to him and leaned toward his ear.

"You faker. You love this!"

He glanced at me, straight jaw and brown

eyes looking older under the brim of the hat, but still the face I had grown up with.

"So do you," he whispered.

FIFTEEN

It was midnight before we trudged up the three flights to Chantel's apartment, exhausted but wired. I was carrying both sleeping bags and two duffles, one with the money.

"How come I have to carry everything?" I said on the second landing.

"Because you're a slavedriver," Chantel said, shoving me playfully against the wall. "A dictator. You should never be allowed to run your own country."

I had worked everybody hard, including myself. After the bonspiel started at eight, the other musicians packed up and left – Andy Larson with a few choice words – but not us. I knew there'd be an intermission, the pavement crowded with smokers, and then the great flood toward the parking lot at the end. In the meantime, I wasn't going to stand around. I paid my admission and went into the arena with one tape and a handful of guitar picks.

Wherever people were, I was there, too.

"This is the best new guitarist in the province," I'd say, flashing the tape. "And tonight only, this guitar pick is worth two dollars off the price of his debut release."

I got some funny looks, but they took the picks.

When people came out, they were greeted by a new, different show. It was dark now. I'd re-parked the truck so it was closer to the front doors, and turned on the headlights. The brilliant white light was behind them but it seemed to beam off their bodies as Daniel and Chantel sang their hearts out, to the crowd and to each other.

It stopped me. It stopped everybody. I don't know what happened, what had changed between the apartment and that piece of pavement. But they weren't those fumbling kids anymore. Black leather and crinkly blond hair faced denim and the acoustic, lips inches apart, biting the words as if they were biting each other.

I see stars when you give it to me, stars when you kiss me, stars make me come...out at night.

Under your sky and under your thumb, keep saying

I'll run, then I'm nailed down again by...starlight.

I got back a lot of guitar picks.

When Chantel opened the door to her apartment, we seemed to explode, tossing jackets and luggage. But I held on to one.

"How much did we make?" Daniel said, grabbing for the duffle.

I held it over my head. "A million bucks."

"Jens! We've got to see, we've got to count it."

Actually, I knew. I'd been counting all along, ticking off cassettes in my head. I was flying.

"It's me," Chantel called suddenly from the kitchen. "He doesn't trust me."

She came back, carrying two beers and a pop.

I unzipped the duffle bag, turned it upside down and shook it. The money fluttered down onto the middle of the floor, 618 dollars in small bills. Chantel squealed and Daniel dropped to his knees, laughing, grabbing it.

"Holy shit! I'm great!"

"No, you're just talented – *I'm* great," I said, tumbling him over with an easy push, my foot on his shoulder.

Chantel's tank top had twisted, showing the white line of her bra strap, and the pink, curvy edge of the tattoo. I was sure it was a heart, with wings.

"And I thought you were just another used car guy," she said, grinning as she handed me a beer.

She gave the other one to Daniel. He glanced at me, a little triumphant, but when he was done, he didn't ask for another.

He argued that Chantel deserved a cut of the money.

"I don't want it. It wasn't my gig. But when it's my turn in the studio, boy, you're going to play your fingers off, for free."

I was sure he would have walked through fire and nails, if that's what she wanted.

"Hey, I was going to ask. Where's the Fender?" Chantel said to Daniel.

"He made me —"

"Leave it at home, safe," I finished for him. He shot me a dark look but I hurried on. "What'd you think of the headlight thing? Every time you moved, the light just rippled — fantastic! You know, if you ever release a CD with Night Drive on it, that should be the cover," I told Daniel excitedly. "You in front of a headlight with the guitar, the grill of the truck behind you..."

When Chantel went to the bathroom, he turned on me.

"I can *talk* now, Jens, by myself."

"And maybe you say too much. You don't tell our shit to a stranger."

"She's not a stranger —"

"I know what she is!" I caught myself, and my voice dropped again. "Daniel, some things you keep in your family."

"Like what?" he demanded.

"Like...I never sent you a birthday card."

"Well, you didn't."

"Okay! But we're guys. Guys don't...do cards." I tried to lighten up. "Am I going to turn on the radio and hear a song about it?"

He straightened in his chair. "So maybe I can't bullshit my way through life. Maybe I write about what matters to me. I'm not ashamed of that."

"And if I made a tape, I wouldn't be ashamed to put my real name on it!"

He glared at me. He opened his mouth to speak, but just then Chantel walked in. "I hate to break up a great party, but I've got to work tomorrow."

I gathered up the money and stuffed it in the bag, which I put on the end of the couch I'd already staked out. Daniel and I moved the coffee table without a word and he spread his sleeping bag out on the floor. Then I went into the bathroom so they could do the goodnight kiss thing. I didn't want to see.

I brushed my teeth, foaming and rinsing and foaming again. I hadn't meant to do that, pick a fight. I didn't even know why I was so aggravated. We'd had a great night — it had been fun being a team. And even my stomach had flipped when I poured it out, all those tens and twenties fluttering to the carpet.

You're leaving tomorrow, I told myself. It's back on the road and back to normal.

The lights were turned low when I came out, and Chantel was gone. Daniel strode past me for his turn in the bathroom. I took off my jeans and left them at the end of the couch; I wasn't going to get caught without my pants.

I crawled in and lay there, thinking. It was strange how things had turned around. Daniel was the shy one but he could show his heart to the whole world. I made a career out of talking to strangers but I couldn't tell my brother anything.

He came back and turned off the last light. The drapes to the glass balcony door were half open and the moon painted the room in white lights and blue shadows. Daniel shuffled out of his pants and slid into his sleeping bag, but he didn't put his head on the pillow. He clutched it to him and laid on top, both arms wrapped around it.

I wanted to tell him I'd meant it, what I told the crowd from the hood of the truck. I thought he was the best guitarist in the province.

"Daniel?"

"What?" He was still mad.

"I'm sorry about the card. I just forgot."

He was silent for a moment. "Well, I wasn't going to get one for you, either. So we're even."

I listened to the hum of the refrigerator, the soft ticking of the cat clock. The couch was against the wall that I knew was her bedroom. I could feel every shift, slight vibrations as she moved in bed. On the floor Daniel rolled over, taking the pillow with him, squirming as he tried to get comfortable. We should all have been dead tired.

I could smell Chantel. It might have been a drift of air from all her perfumes in the bathroom, or a trace she'd left on the couch. Or maybe she'd pressed the scent on Daniel when she'd kissed him.

I should have taken care of myself in the shower, followed the fantasy all the way — safe, silent, fast. But even the thought made me sting. I wasn't a kid anymore. I couldn't help listening to Daniel breathe, wondering if he'd fall asleep before me.

I must have dozed off. I woke up as he walked past, a glimpse of his bare, sinewy legs like a ghost. The moon wasn't shining in anymore; the room was all shades of gray. I blinked, waiting to hear him go into the bathroom. Instead there was a shuffling sound, his hand brushing wood. Then the faintest click of the knob as he opened Chantel's door and went in.

On the other side of the wall, she giggled.

My skin was burning. They'd planned this. She'd planned it. Daniel wouldn't have gone without an invitation. In plain English.

I felt the tremor as he walked over to the bed, then the low murmur of her voice, no words but I could imagine. I could imagine it all. How it'd look as she threw back the covers to him, the curve from her waist to her round hips, the winged heart over her soft, heavy breasts.

They were getting louder, forgetting themselves, excited whispers and rushes of sound. They both had smoky voices. I could see the silences in vivid detail, mouths and hands, and all the parts they could touch.

My brother moaned.

Oh, God. I couldn't listen to this. But I couldn't stop, either. My erection was straining against my shorts, and I could hear my own breath now.

This is sad, Jens. This is so fucking pathetic.

I hated that she could do this to me. Even as I took myself out, even as I rode the fantasy of that pink mouth and painted hair, peeled away her black, trampy clothes in my mind and made her see stars, on the bed, against the wall, on the floor of the Rosetown Raiders locker room.

The girl who said I had a peasant's body was Marie Gagnon. I was in grade eleven and I was aware of every female in my school and on the planet, but there was something about French girls that made me stare. That shiny dark hair and brown eyes, black eyelashes that could brush you off in a flutter.

Marie Gagnon wore thick eyeliner, black on top, blue underneath. When she wore lipstick it was dark burgundy, red so deep it looked purple, a color that could mark your skin and clothes forever. There was a group of about ten girls who came to all the Raiders games, then hung around after to talk when we came out.

It was no secret that Marie was waiting for Jeff Styrchak, grade twelve and six feet two, a tight end who could barely remember the plays from one game to the next. Marie was not interested in football.

"In uniform and on the floor, that's how I'd like his tight end," I heard her tell her friends once. They burst into laughter.

But Jeff had been dating the same girl for three years. He said hi to Marie on the way to his car. So when she hung around she talked to me. Away from her group, I thought she was nice. I'd spend all week thinking of something to say to make her laugh. She had a car and sometimes she'd drive me home. We could steam up the windows pretty good, saying goodnight. I thought she liked me.

One day in school I overheard her telling her girlfriends she wanted to get into the Raiders locker room, just to see it.

"In the dark, that's how you'd like to see it!" somebody hooted.

"Face it, Marie, Jeff's not going to give you the tour," another girl said.

Marie smiled wickedly. "That's why you have a second string. You know, alternate players..."

"Not the Chocolate King!"

"Yeah, but he's got a peasant's body," she grinned, "and it's in the right uniform."

I stopped liking Marie Gagnon. But I didn't stop wanting her. After the next home game I found a way to take her back to the locker room once everyone had gone. I was still wearing my jersey over my jeans, a three-pack of Trojan condoms in my back pocket.

Marie was excited to be there, even though I'd left the lights off and it was too dark to really see anything. Lockers and benches, the dusky smell of sweat — it meant nothing to me.

"This is one of my fantasies," she whispered against my ear, then she bit it.

And my neck, and my lips. She pulled up her own sweater and my jersey, and her bare skin and soft breasts were a hot shock against me. I was bursting out of my clothes. I threw our coats onto the floor.

I wanted to forgive. Wrapped up by her, breathing into her silky hair, strength and pleasure driving me in raw thrusts, I was ready to forgive and forget and love.

"Oh," she moaned under me. "Oh, Jeff."

That's when I started to say it, in my mind at first but over and over, the power of those two terrible words rushing through me, driving me harder, until I couldn't stop, until I gasped it in her ear.

"French slut."

Supernova, against a black, black sky.

◆

I was a mess. There was a box of tissues on the table beside the couch. I cleaned myself up and pulled the sleeping bag around me again, heavy with relief. But maybe it was the wrong thing. Like water over a dam the feeling flooded through me, a scalding wave that squeezed my throat shut.

I just wanted somebody. Somebody who liked me right now and today. I was trying so hard. I wanted somebody to hold me and say it'd be okay.

My chest was throbbing where Daniel had hit me.

Breathe, Jens.

I opened my mouth and took a careful, thin breath, like that first one on the lawn. Then another, and another, controlling it.

See, it's okay. You're okay.

There were no more sounds from the other room. I realized there hadn't been for awhile. I wondered if Daniel would come back, and if I should pretend to be asleep when he did.

I heard the door open and decided fast, sliding down, my face in the crook of my arm, but high enough so that I could still see through my half-closed eyes.

Chantel sauntered out wearing Daniel's T-shirt, the edge of it brushing the bottom of her white panties. She glanced at me on her way to the kitchen. Her cigarettes were on the counter and she lit one, a yellow burst in the darkness. Then she walked over to the balcony doors and stood looking out, blowing smoke against the glass.

She was completely unconcerned, almost serene.

"I guess you got what you wanted," I said.

She was so startled she dropped her cigarette, then crouched, scrambling to find it before it burned the carpet. I pushed up onto my elbow, my lower half safely hidden in the sleeping bag.

"It was a pretty smart move to get in on the ground floor," I continued, my voice quiet and even.

Chantel found the cigarette and stood up, facing me. She folded her arms self-consciously over her chest but she held her ground, legs long and white. I expected her to defend herself, maybe even say that she loved him or something.

"You have a problem with women, don't you, Jens?" she said. "I mean, you want us, but you don't like us."

It caught me off guard, a slap. My face was on fire.

"Maybe...maybe it's just you —"

"I've been trying to figure it out," she said, shaking her head. "You were raised the same, by the same parents. But somehow he's the only one who can communicate, who can have a relationship..."

"He didn't talk until he was four years old! They thought he was retarded!"

She looked at me, her features cold and clean without makeup. "And he thinks you're a god."

She strode out, the long ash from her cigarette blowing off, falling onto the carpet.

SIXTEEN

I woke up and it was Monday. The realization ran through me like a cramp. I sat up on the couch, my heart beating quickly, the apartment silent and still around me. Through the balcony glass I could see the sky, a solid cover of clouds that had swept in through the night. It would rain today.

I shrugged out of my cocoon and went for another shower. I hated to use up the hot water but I really needed it. I felt grimy.

Shaved and dressed, I rolled up both sleeping bags, thinking about money. The Starling show plus what we'd made last night totaled 898 dollars. If we added in the Fender money – less what we'd used – we were at 1,248. Halfway there.

Except Daniel didn't want to spend the

Fender, and I didn't know if I could convince Kruse to settle for fifty percent. And I still had phone calls to make. For a second I felt it, my life snapping at my heels. Today was Monday.

I yanked the knots on the sleeping bag tight. I had to stay focused, keep my priorities straight. When you've got the ball, you just run, you don't look behind you.

I took the two bedrolls and the duffle full of money, making sure the apartment didn't lock behind me. When I pushed out through the main door with my shoulder, a gust of icy wind took my breath away. Damn, it was cold. The temperature must have dropped during the night. I felt an uneasy tug. No matter what I'd promised Mom, I hadn't been following the weather reports. It was lucky we'd slept at Chantel's. This morning would have been...a shock.

I hurried to unlock the back of the truck, wincing as a new blast stung my face. The empty cereal box was still there and I put all the money into it, carefully reclosing the lid before I tucked it in with the food supplies. I figured any thief with half a brain would take the guitars and leave the Lucky Charms. I grabbed a box of Vegetable Thins on my way out. I wasn't going to eat any more of Chantel's food.

I let myself into the apartment quietly, and

was glad to hear the shower running. But was it for her or him? Down the hall, the door to her bedroom was ajar. I crept toward it and eased it open.

My brother was stretched out under a pastel pink sheet, one arm under his head, smoking a cigarette. He looked at me in alarm, then seemed to catch himself. He took a defiant drag.

"Hi," he said, and grinned.

"Get dressed," I said. "We have to go."

He sat up. "I want to stay another day."

My guts pulled tight. I'd known this would happen. "Look, we're out here to do a job —"

"And we're way ahead. I'm ahead! Last night was six hundred bucks, Jens. I deserve...a day off."

"Did she ask you?"

"No. But she'll say yes," he said triumphantly.

I looked away, then back at him. "Daniel, just because she lays you doesn't mean she loves you," I said softly.

His face contorted, a quick spasm, as if I'd hit him.

"You're...jealous." There was an ashtray on the night table and he stabbed out the cigarette, breaking it in half. "You don't know her, you don't even like her, but you can't stand that it's me! Somebody wants me!" His voice dropped to a hush. "You don't know what we've got. I'd do anything for her."

I could feel my pulse in my temples, my throat.

"Then you go ahead and ask her if you can stay," I said, pulling the door shut as I left. I went into the living room, still in my jacket, and ripped the top off the Vegetable Thins. I stared out the balcony window, chewing through the dry, spicy crackers one after another.

The water had stopped running. I'd expected Chantel to go into the bedroom but when I heard her footsteps pass behind me to the kitchen, I held my breath. I really didn't want this chance, but I had it.

"You could have made coffee," she said, "since you were up."

I was suddenly in the doorway of the galley kitchen, blocking it. Chantel's hair was twisted in a towel and she was wearing a long bathrobe. Wrapped up like that, bare face and neck in all that white, she looked more naked than last night.

"I know you think I'm shit," I said, my voice low so only she would hear. "Maybe you're right. Maybe I've got...a problem. Maybe every single guy in the world has got a problem. Okay! But that doesn't mean we don't have hearts. That we don't feel everything just as bad, just as hard as you do..."

She looked shaken, surprised. She tried to speak but I kept going.

"Daniel's a kid," I said again. "Yeah, he's talented, he's sweet, but he's a little piece of your life. And he's going to make you all of his. Then what are you going to do? Think about it. Are you ready for that?"

She bit her lip.

I turned away. "Tell Daniel I'm out in the truck."

I seemed to sit there for a long time, shivering even after the heat began to blow. My stomach felt like a solid block of those awful crackers. I didn't know if I'd done the right thing.

Finally my brother came out carrying the last duffle, shoulders hunched against the wind. His face was dark with stubble. He hadn't stayed to shave.

I watched him get in, pulling the big bag onto his knees instead of dropping it on the floor.

"Just go," he said.

"What happened?"

"Just fucking drive!" He turned his face to the window.

I wanted to touch him, maybe put my hand on his shoulder. But I knew he was spinning, like me the day I threw all his stuff out into the hallway. Daniel had his tornadoes on the inside.

I couldn't leave Easton fast enough, not even filling up on gas. On the highway, I took the first junction north.

The landscape was changing, flat farmland giving way to brush and trees. Lake country. I had made up my mind to go to Thompson, Manitoba. Far up in the northern part of the province, it was actually a small city, and one of the last places you could get to by road. Built entirely on nickel mining, it struck me as a place of bars and money, but too remote to attract live entertainment. I wanted to take Daniel where the audience was hungry, satellite TV or not.

In my heart, I knew it was crazy. We'd been drifting north since we'd set out from Ile-des-Sapins but it was still a five-hour drive. We'd burn a tank of gas each way. Yet I'd decided I would make my phone calls, to Five Star Ford and my landlord, only after we'd reached Thompson and booked a gig. I wasn't stalling, only...setting up. Like a magic number. If I could get my brother a gig in Thompson, I could phone anybody in the world.

"Where are we going?" Daniel said. It was his first sound in an hour. He was slouched against the door, the bag still on his knees, hiding under it.

"North. I thought we'd see what's up this way." I wasn't going to tell him yet how far.

He shrugged. "When are we going to phone home?"

"We're not. Not today," I blurted. If Five Star Ford had called Dad, I didn't want to know about it yet. I had my plan.

"But Mom said —"

"I told Dad it'd be soon. That doesn't mean today." I took a breath and let it out slowly. "I've got it under control."

Then it started to snow. It was so soft at first, tiny flakes that melted as soon as they hit the windshield. Daniel looked at me.

"It's rain," I said.

"I'm not sleeping in it."

"For Christ's sake, it's not even noon. We'll drive right through it. Here," I snapped on the radio. "Listen for the weather."

Within minutes we caught it: Heavy snowfall warning for southern Manitoba, winds gusting to seventy kilometers an hour.

"That's south," I said. "We're driving north. We just have to keep going north and we'll be okay."

But I could feel the wind picking up, the pressure as it buffeted the truck. The flakes were larger now, fluttering against the windshield, swirling in eddies across the highway. I was gripping the steering wheel with both hands.

It couldn't storm. We only had our light jackets and no gloves and I didn't want to spend the money on a motel. And we had to get to Thompson. Before somebody reported the truck missing, or stolen.

So stop at the next town, I argued with myself. If you're that worried, just call.

But I needed a...boost. I needed to do something right, get the adrenaline going before I could face anything hard. There was twelve hundred dollars in a cereal box but that was yesterday's success. Today I needed another hit.

Daniel finally shuffled the bag onto the floor and put his feet on it, making me glance at him. He looked pale and tired, as if he was sick. My mind did a strange sideways leap.

"Did you use a condom?" I asked abruptly.

"Oh, Jesus, Jens...!"

"Just tell me – did you?"

"Yes!" He wouldn't look at me. Even from the side I could see him burn, face and neck flushing.

"So I'm not...an expert. Like you. But I'm not stupid!" His voice dipped. "She had a whole box."

His hat was on the dashboard and he reached for it, took it onto his lap. My brother wasn't deaf, and he wasn't blind, either. But he'd written a song for this girl.

I was sorry I'd brought Chantel up, brought

her into the truck with us. The air seemed suddenly heavy. Daniel was leaning into the door again, clutching his hat. I squeezed the accelerator a little harder, wondering how you ever knew if you'd done the right thing.

"You have a problem, don't you, Jens?"

We're halfway there, I thought. I'm halfway to pulling this off and if I sold fifty percent in two days, I can get the other fifty percent in two more. It's another twelve hundred dollars, maybe only a thousand, if I can work Kruse right.

"You were raised the same, by the same parents. But somehow..."

Five hundred bucks a day! I only had to sell fifty tapes a day!

"...he's the only one..."

A highway sign – sixteen kilometers to Swan River. Thank God. It was a town I'd heard of, big enough for a gas station and a restaurant. The pangs were digging at my insides again and I wanted something real and hot. A burger and fries.

"We're going to stop in Swan," I said. "We'll get you some lunch."

I was watching the road, trying not to be hypnotized by the snow that was coming straight at us, driving wildly at the windshield without touching it.

"Why'd you tell me to ask Chantel if we

could stay, when you only wanted to go?" Daniel said.

It wasn't an accusation, but he was waiting for an answer.

"Because I knew what she'd say," I said finally.

He was silent the rest of the way.

It got worse closer to Swan River. Freezing slush was piling up around the bush, layering on the asphalt. I slowed down, even though I didn't want to.

The pumps were self-serve. Filling the tank, I turned my back to the wind, but it still bit through my light coat, my hands growing numb as I tried to squeeze the fuel in as fast as possible. It was a relief to get inside the little restaurant. Daniel followed me in and strode past to the restroom. I paid for the gas and ordered the burgers.

I leaned against the counter, watching the white rage through the window, chewing my lip.

It's only weather, I told myself.

"How far you going?" The man at the lunch counter looked so much like Dad, big shoulders in a gunmetal blue jacket, light brown hair running gray. My legs felt suddenly weak. I wanted to sit down beside him.

"We have to get to Thompson," I said.

He shook his head. "It's been upgraded to a

blizzard warning. You'll be lucky to get to The Pas."

"Did they close Highway 10?"

"Not yet, but they probably will. You shouldn't risk it," he finished quietly.

I was stretched, half of me still running inside, desperate to beat the storm. The other half of me wanted to stop now and stay right here.

"Jens," Daniel called. He was out of the bathroom and looking at a bulletin board by the doorway, papered with notices. He unpinned a business card. "This is where we should go. Rene's — it's a guitar bar. In The Pas."

I looked at the man who looked like my father.

"I can make it to The Pas," I said.

In the truck, I gave the boxtop tray with the food to Daniel to hold until I got us back on the highway. But the smell was driving me crazy — small town burgers are the best in the world. I'd gotten a double, with the cheese and bacon layered in the middle. As soon as I was up to cruising speed I had it open, bit into it gratefully, ketchup trailing down the side of my hand and I didn't even care. I had the cardboard cup of super-large fries nestled between my legs. If I steered with my forearm, I could reach those, too.

You're not failing, I told myself, even if you

don't make it to Thompson. You just have to get him a gig. That's all that matters.

I wound up eating Daniel's burger, too. He said he wasn't hungry.

SEVENTEEN

For three hours we crept along Highway 10. I dropped speed to eighty klicks, then sixty, then fifty. I had both hands on the wheel, my shoulders knotting as I struggled to see through the white blur all around us. I had about fifteen meters of visibility and the windshield was crusted with frozen slush. Dad had taught me to feel the road through the tires, but patches of ice still caught me by surprise, sudden fish-tail slides that made Daniel grip his handrest. But he didn't say anything. Neither of us felt like talking.

Once I saw a flashing red and blue light ahead of us, and I went cold inside. I didn't want to be stopped for any reason. To my relief it was an RCMP cruiser standing guard by a car that had gone into the ditch. I gave them a wide berth and kept going.

Five o'clock, I told myself. If I called the dealership before five o'clock it'd be considered the same day. Nobody could call that theft.

But I wondered how soon a vehicle went into the RCMP computer system after it was reported.

The day dragged on. The storm made it seem later than it was, dusk that never became night. At 3:45 I finally saw the overhead four-way stop, swinging and bobbing in the wind, and we limped into The Pas. I felt as if I'd crawled the whole way on my hands and knees.

Okay, Jens. You got here and you're okay. You can phone now.

"What's the address of that guitar bar?" I asked.

Daniel looked at me in disbelief. "We've got to call home. They're going to be worried..."

"We will! Right after. Don't be such a suckhole." I heard myself, meaner than I meant, but I couldn't stop it. "You're the one who wanted to come here, so we're here."

The map legend had said The Pas was a city of between five and ten thousand, but you never would have known it. A few cars rolled along cautiously and the occasional pedestrian hurried by, bundled and desperate to get somewhere else. The streets were worse than the highway — deep ruts of dirty snow laid over ice. I drove up and down the main drags, trying not to stop, swearing under my breath.

At one traffic light I got stuck. I sat revving the engine, wheels spinning helplessly, even though I knew better. When you lose traction, you're supposed to take your foot off the accelerator and try to creep forward instead of digging yourself in deeper. But you panic, afraid to stop moving because then you'll really be stuck. You think if you just gun it harder you'll catch a piece of the road.

This time it worked. I surged into the intersection at last, relieved.

"There it is," Daniel said, pointing.

Rene's Guitar Bar was a sliver of a storefront between a lunch cafe and a space for lease. The painted sign over the door looked old and weathered but in the window hung the outline of an electric guitar in blue neon. The rest of the bar was dark.

I pulled up to the curb and cut the engine. The sudden stillness felt good and I wanted to just sit for a minute. But I couldn't stop. It was four o'clock.

Daniel followed me onto the sidewalk, his hat pulled down, jacket open. The snow came over the tops of our runners. In seconds my ears and face were stinging.

I grabbed the door handle. It was locked.

Shit! I peered through the window in the metal door and thought I saw a light burning in the back. I started to pound on the door with the side of my fist.

"Wait in the truck!" I yelled at Daniel over the wind. But he hung beside me stubbornly, one hand on his hat, the other jammed into his pocket. My cold fist was aching but still I stood there, whipped by wind and snow, hammering on the metal door. Somebody had to come. It was four o'clock and I didn't know what else to do.

The door finally swung open.

"What the hell do you want? I'm closed."

The man was huge. Taller than me, bigger than me, he was solid from his wide shoulders down, thick arms and legs like tree trunks. His long hair had probably once been dark but now it was mostly silver, pulled back in a ponytail. Gold rings on his fingers, black leather jacket. He looked like an aging biker.

"Hi, how are you today?" I said, trying to edge my way in. But he blocked the entire doorway.

"It's a freakin' blizzard. I'm cold."

I laughed nervously. "Well, yeah. So are we, actually. Can...can we come in for a minute? I'd like to talk to you...about the bar."

"What about my bar?"

"I think I know a way to improve business," I said quickly.

He hesitated, as if he couldn't believe what he was seeing. Snow was blowing in from behind us. At last he backed away.

"One minute," he said.

The sudden warmth of the dark, narrow room made me dizzy. In the mirror behind the bar I caught a glimpse of two snowmen — me and Daniel. There was space for about eight little tables and, at one end, a raised platform with a drum kit set up. But when my eyes adjusted I realized this place wasn't about the bar or even the stage. It was built for one wall.

I stared. I didn't count, but there must have been fourteen or fifteen guitars hanging there, an incredible spread of color and shapes, wood and metal. Fender, Gibson, Marshall, Rickenbacker. A solid steel guitar shone like mercury. There were acoustics and electrics and some that looked as if they'd been caught halfway between the two.

I lost my brother. He took off his snowy hat, clutched it in both hands as he drifted to the wall, lips parted.

"What about my bar?" Rene said again.

I jumped right into my spiel — who we were and where we were from, how Daniel could improve business because people stayed longer and drank more when there was live entertainment. Standing next to that wall, the words sounded hollow even to me. You fool, Jens, was all I could think. You used car guy.

And still I kept going, stumbling over myself, digging in deeper.

"...and he took first place in the solo guitar category at SunJam. It's a provincial comp —"

"I know what it is. Milky bastards."

"Hey, you're absolutely right! That's what we said, too, but it led to this recording..." I fumbled for the cassette. Damn! I'd left it in the truck again.

Rene plucked a CD from a display on the bar that I hadn't noticed before. His picture was on it, with the steel guitar, and full band backup. *Mercy Please*.

"We've already got a house band," he said. I could see it in his eyes: his bar, his band, his music.

"Please," I lowered my voice, "you don't have to pay him anything."

"You're Bourbon Ray," Daniel blurted. He was looking at Rene now, staring at him hard, as if he was a ghost who'd disappear. It was the first time he'd taken his eyes off the wall of guitars. "You...you opened for Muddy Waters in the seventies. At the concert hall in Winnipeg. You were a Blues Brat."

Rene bit his lip as if he'd been caught in a lie, but he couldn't stop the grin. It lit up his rough face.

"August 25th, 1977. Me and Dave McLean and Gord Kidder. Yeah, we were the Brats."

"Big Dave McLean," Daniel repeated in a hushed voice. "He was a mentor to Colin James."

Rene was nodding, truly smiling now. He started toward Daniel, toward the wall. "You a history student, little man?"

"I'm...a student."

Rene unhooked a battered black acoustic from the wall. The finish on the wood had been worn right off over the frets. He held it out to my brother. Daniel was squeezing his hat. He looked down at the guitar as if he was afraid of it. Rene made a small movement, almost a shrug, and at last Daniel reached out for it.

My heart sped up. Play "Night Drive," I prayed. Show him, Daniel.

There was no shoulder strap attached. Daniel pulled out a chair and put his foot on it, setting the guitar over his thigh. He dug a pick out of his pocket, then looked hesitantly at Rene once more.

"My hands are cold..."

Bourbon Ray nodded patiently. Daniel

strummed a few times. It sounded tuned to me. *Play*, Daniel.

It wasn't "Night Drive." It was true blues, Waters or Dixon or one of those old guys, notes tripping over themselves as they walked, rhythm so lazy I couldn't find the beat.

Bourbon Ray could. His foot began to tap. Soon he started to hum and halfway through he couldn't stand it anymore. *"Well my mother told my father/Just before I was born..."* His voice seemed to rumble out from below his belt. *"...gonna be a rollin' stone..."*

And that's how it started. One song led to another. An electric came down off the wall, and a bass. When Bourbon Ray took over the strings, Daniel stood, swaying with the beat but rapt, as if he was memorizing every movement, every quivering sound. The guitar pick disappeared in his huge hand, but Bourbon Ray was liquid fire.

They looked so different, a silver-haired giant and my long-legged stringy little brother. But as they passed the guitars back and forth, watched and listened and finally played together, I knew. They spoke the same language.

I had a headache, dull pain throbbing in my temples and behind my eyes. I stood at the bar, shifting from foot to foot. Did we have a booking or didn't we?

It was twenty to five. They were between songs, talking about people I'd never heard of and the Chess recordings, the kind of stuff my brother used to bore me with all the time. Now his face was shining.

"Daniel," I interrupted.

He looked over, as if he was surprised I was still there, that I existed at all.

The bar was too small to be private. I tugged my brother into the men's room.

"Ask him," I said.

"What?"

"Ask him! If you can have a gig."

Daniel looked dumbfounded. "Jens...that's Bourbon Ray. The man is a legend and he's actually *talking* to me. We're jamming. I'm playing his guitars!"

"Daniel —"

"I'm lucky to even be here."

The pain in my temples was harder now, it had begun to pound. "If you're not going to ask, then we've got to go. Right now. There are other places..."

"No! Not this time. I pawned the Fender. I stood on your truck like an idiot — a freak show — because you wanted it. Now I finally get something for me..."

"What are you talking about? It's all for you. There's a thousand bucks sitting in that truck—"

"So why don't you *eat* it? Shove it down your own throat like you shove it down mine!"

I hit him, a wild swing with the side of my forearm that caught him hard across the ear. He stumbled back into a stall door. It blew in against the metal wall with a bang.

The bathroom door burst open. Rene knocked me against the wall, pinned me to it with one big arm, the light switch digging into my back. His eyes were icy blue.

"Don't wreck my place," Bourbon Ray said.

"I'm going," I gasped.

After a few seconds, he released me. I started for the door. Daniel was still standing in the stall, holding his ear, glaring at me.

"I hate your guts," he whispered.

I kept going. On the street, I leaned into the wind. It was cool against my throbbing head. I plowed along the sidewalk, sliding, stumbling in the snow.

So I didn't get to Thompson. So I didn't get Daniel a gig. I could still fix this! I still had the ball and I could run with it – today, right now.

In the sports bar at the end of the street, there was a phone cubicle at the back of the room. I got a handful of change from the bartender. I was trying not to shake.

"Kruse Studios," he answered.

"This is Jens Friesen."

"Jens! Just the man I want to..."

"Well, good," I cut him off. "Because I've got something to say to you, too. I've been doing some investigating and I don't think you've been fair to my family. I think the deal you offered my parents was about twice the going rate, and you knew they'd take it because they'd do anything for their kid. And maybe Daniel's not anything special to you but he doesn't deserve..."

"I think the world of your brother," Kruse broke in. "He's an exciting talent, and a hell of a songwriter."

I was stunned.

"I...I've been trying to reach you all day, to apologize for Friday," the producer hurried on. "I said things I didn't mean. Maybe we all did. But I want you to know that I'd really appreciate the opportunity to keep working with Daniel."

I didn't know what to think. Kruse was saying he wanted the contract in effect again, but I hadn't even finished my speech.

"What about the money?"

He laughed, a thin and nervous sound. "Well, I think that can be resolved. I...heard from Home Grown Music today and they're very interested in a songwriting contract with Daniel — not as a recording artist, but as a writer. They're not a big label but I'm sure you know what an important step this is. After all, he *is* only sixteen years old."

All Daniel had to do was record whatever he wrote and send it to Home Grown. Kruse would handle all the negotiations, as his agent.

"Did you tell our mom and dad?"

Kruse hesitated. "You know, I wanted to talk to you first. Daniel's...passionate. Hey, that's a good thing. It means he cares about what he does. But I know he was upset on Friday." He took a breath. "He really looks up to you."

I had the ball. I had it in my hands. And there was no game.

"Mr. Kruse," I said quietly, "I'm sure Daniel will be thrilled."

I hung up the phone and sat down at the bar. I didn't get up for a long time.

EIGHTEEN

It was about eleven o'clock when I knocked the stool over as I slid off. Bending down to get it, the room tipped. I grabbed the edge of the bar so I wouldn't go, too. Only a few people looked.

When I straightened up, the bartender put his hand over my forearm. His name was Martin and we were friends. I'd spent a lot of time telling him how to make a perfect omelet.

"You're not going to drive, Jens," he said.

I was touched. I felt heat behind my eyes and the sudden terror that it might be tears.

"You're a straight-up guy, Martin," I said, and tried to turn away. But he kept me pinned easily with my arm on the bar. I was amazed. I was bigger than he was.

"How are you going to get home?" he said.

He meant it. He wouldn't let me go without an answer.

"My brother's...down the street," I said.

The bartender finally released his grip. "All right. You make sure he takes you, now."

I got as far as the door before I looked back. "I'm really sorry, Martin." I meant about the stool. "God, I'm so sorry."

I pushed outside and stumbled into winter. It had stopped snowing but the wind was still blowing harder than ever. One corner of my brain kept telling me to do up my jacket, but the rest of me was completely absorbed with walking, just staying upright, one hand on the storefronts and buildings, getting through the jagged drifts crusted by ice.

It was a long street, longer than I remembered. My insides started to slosh, then churn. It had been a bad idea to switch from beer to rum, and finally Scotch. Glenkinchie, just like Sy.

I'd lied to Martin. I couldn't go home. For seven months I'd stayed away even when things seemed good, because they weren't good enough. And now it was Monday. Today I was a thief. And a liar. And a bastard. My brother hated me and I deserved it.

I had to stop between two buildings and throw up. Afterwards, I leaned against one of the walls, my forehead on the bricks, and closed my eyes. I felt as if I'd been running and running for years.

Just a little farther, Jens. There's one more thing you have to do.

Into the wind again, staggering forward.

I felt the music before I heard it, through the boards of the buildings that held me up. When I reached the window with the blue neon, it was throbbing with kick-ass guitar, vibrating with drums. I leaned on the glass, looking inside.

It didn't take many people to make the little bar look full; the band itself seemed to take up half the room. Bourbon Ray was out front, huge and black and silver. He was playing the steel guitar. There was a guy on harp beside him and the drummer in the back. Red and blue lights made them all seem magical.

I didn't see Daniel until he moved. He was tucked in tight on that little stage, almost in the middle of the circle of musicians. He was playing an electric bass. I'd never seen him play one but I didn't doubt he was doing it, smoking the strings and making it run. Over the last few days I'd come to believe my brother could play anything.

His hat was pulled down so low you couldn't see his eyes. He leaned back and yet into the strings, the guitar an extension of his body. He was flying. And the whole room was loving him.

It took a lot to push in the door. The warm, smoke-filled room seemed to burn my skin. Walking through the music was like swimming, it was so thick and loud, but I went straight to the bar, amazingly straight, and handed over my truck keys to the girl behind the counter.

I nodded at Daniel. "These are for my brother," I said carefully. "Tell him I said to eat his cereal."

She looked at me curiously. "I'm sorry," I told her. I meant that she had to look after the keys.

She must have seen something in my face because she touched my hand. I felt the burning rush again – up my throat and behind my eyes. I pulled away and walked out. I hoped Daniel hadn't seen me.

I was almost grateful for the wind, something to lean into, to fight against. The sidewalk was less slippery here or maybe I was walking better. I didn't have to hang onto the wall so I jammed my hands into my jacket pockets. I was in a hurry. The only alcohol I had left was in my bloodstream. It wouldn't last forever.

There were two more streets, then the turn-off for the highway. Number 10, to Thompson.

People would say I'd done a terrible thing, leaving Daniel. But I knew his friends would look after him tonight and I'd told him where to find the money. Tomorrow he'd call Mom and Dad, if he hadn't already. After that he'd have Mogen Kruse and Home Grown and God knew what else. Daniel would be okay. He had the kind of problems that could be fixed.

It had started to snow again, not the big white flakes we'd seen on the way in, but small ice crystals that blasted me like sand. It should have stung but it didn't. I wasn't even cold anymore. I could feel the wind buffeting my body in waves but mostly I was just tired. Really tired.

I had reached the highway. I had to get close to the sign to read it. At first I thought it was the snow, but then I realized everything was blurry. Okay. All I had to see was the road in front of me.

My body was starting to feel light and warm now, as if I was floating. I didn't have to worry about cars. It was midnight Monday in the middle of a snowstorm. No one was out. I didn't have to worry about Mom. She'd be upset but she had Daniel. And Dad. I was sorry about the garage. Oh, God, I was sorry. But I was giving him this, the way to explain it. *He was drunk, he was confused, he just got lost...*

I seemed to fall for a long time, minutes from the stumble to the slow pitch forward, the highway coming up to me, gray and white.

There was no pain when I hit, no shock of contact. It was like watching someone else, from the inside. And I was so comfortable, relieved to finally stop. Jack Lahanni had been wrong. I did have the sense to lie down.

My eyes were open. I was just looking at the highway, watching the snow swirl across it, when I saw the light. I felt the vibration like buzzing. I could even hear it. I was so calm and tired that nothing could scare me.

Like watching a movie I saw the truck swerve around me, then swing over suddenly to compensate, then begin to skid. It spun around 360 degrees before it plunged nose-first off the asphalt.

The back tires were still spinning when the realization hit me. That was my truck. My truck was in the ditch. Alarm shot through my numb body and I pushed up on my arms. I knew who had the keys.

I staggered to my feet and stumbled over, my wooden legs gathering strength with every step. I charged down into the ditch into knee-deep snow and yanked open the driver's door. Daniel threw up his arms.

"Don't hit me! I'm sorry!"

"For God's sake, are you hurt?"

"No, I swear! Jens, I'm sorry."

It was all I could do to get him to turn off the

engine and climb out of the cab. I tugged him over to the sheltered side of the truck, out of the wind, and for a minute we just leaned there, catching our breath. I couldn't believe he'd come after me.

"Daniel...why would you take the truck?"

"You left me the keys. I saw you in the bar. As soon as the set was over, I ran out after you but I couldn't catch up."

"*Scheisskopf!* You could've been killed!"

He was looking at me through narrowed eyes. "Why were you lying on the highway? You...scared me."

For a brief second I imagined it through my own eyes, that it was me driving, seeing him on the side of the road. I would have gone into the ditch, too.

"I fell," I said.

"And you just lay there?!"

It was all gone. The adrenaline and the alcohol and the panic — everything that was holding me up. I slumped against the truck, clinging to it. I wanted to go to sleep.

"Jens, what's the matter?"

"I don't feel so good," I muttered. "You have to walk back, get a tow truck."

"No, you're sick. I can't leave you here."

"Just —"

But he was gone, around the back. In a daze,

I slid down the side of the truck to my knees. I felt the tremor as he opened the hatch, and other movements as he rattled around inside.

Then he was back. I could see his runners in front of me, blue and black Nikes in the snow.

"Jens, get up." I could hear the alarm in his voice. "I cleared out a space. We'll sleep in the truck."

I shook my head numbly.

"It's not as cold out of the wind. And we'll share heat."

I didn't answer. He grabbed my arm. "Get up! I mean it!"

He couldn't lift me, couldn't even get me to my feet, but he was trying. Even now, after everything. The heat rushed to my face, scalded my eyes. I had nothing to give him anymore. I'd tried and tried but there was nothing I could do to make it up.

"Damn it, Jens," he muttered, struggling with me. "What's the matter with you?!"

"I treated you like shit." The words tumbled out, thick and raw. "You trusted me and I just wanted you to hurt, to pay because I was so screwed up and you weren't. And it wasn't your fault. You didn't deserve any of it. I'd take it back if I could – every rotten day, I swear." I touched my cold fingers to my burning forehead. "It's okay to hate me. I hate me, too. But

I'm sorry. God, I'm sorry."

I couldn't get up, couldn't even raise my head. All my life I'd been bigger than him.

His runners were still. He'd stopped pulling on me. For an awful second there was nothing, only the sound of wind howling around the truck. At last he gripped the shoulder of my jacket, held it so tight I could feel his knuckles digging into me.

"It's okay, Jens."

Three words, but the relief flooded through me, almost swamped me in a wave. His Nikes were swimming in front of me.

"Okay," I whispered back. And I used his arm to pull myself up.

/NINETEEN

I woke up warm. Daniel had wriggled over in his sleep, and now his back was against my shoulder. With our clothes and jackets and the sleeping bags and each other, we'd made it through the night. My face felt sunburned; I knew that was frostbite, but when I checked my fingers and toes I could move them easily. I'd gotten into the truck in time.

And that's when it sank in what I'd almost done. I was suddenly weak and shaken. Yeah, I'd been drunk and sick of myself, but I'd set out knowing I couldn't walk to Thompson. I'd set out thinking only of myself, where I hurt.

You've got a problem, Jens, I told myself. And I'd almost given it to my whole family, the people I loved most. I'd done some stupid and selfish things, but none came close to that. And there was no quick fix, nothing I could win or earn that would make me feel better the way I needed it — right now. All I could do was live it out day by day.

I could feel Daniel breathe, a faint vibration against my shoulder. Last night I'd told him he was going to be famous. He'd listened intently as I gave him the news about Home Grown. He had me repeat the phone call word for word, but he wasn't as excited as I thought he'd be.

I'd told him a lot — that I didn't have a job anymore, or this truck or even a place to live. It was hard. I'd spent seven months building that cardboard man. I'd almost believed in him, too.

All Daniel said was, "Come home. Dad won't be mad."

"It's not about Dad." As soon as I said it, I knew it was true. Everything I'd done, everything I'd wanted, had been to make me feel better.

"I need you to come home," Daniel said quietly. "I can't take it anymore. They're on me all the time and..."

"You're their kid. They love you."

"But they're just parents."

And I was his brother. It wasn't like being a friend. We could hurt each other harder, or help each other more. Three words from him had made me feel almost new, as if I could start again.

The windows of the box were tinted. I knew it was morning outside but I couldn't move yet.

I would be nineteen in seven days. My mother was hardly a year older than that when she'd had me. She'd been a kid. For a minute I just held that revelation, felt it fill up my chest. The things I'd done to Daniel had been on purpose, and he'd still forgiven me. I knew what it meant to get another chance.

The air around me was dim and close.

"It's okay, Mom," I whispered.

At last I twisted onto my stomach and gently pushed the hatch door. We'd left it unlocked for air, but it was on a spring. It flew open, shaking the truck.

Daniel flipped over, startled awake. He looked at me and then outside, blinking at the brilliant blue sky and melting snow.

His guitars and amps were all on the side of the highway. As we loaded them back in, I was amazed that he would have risked this.

He was inside the truck, finding space for the things I passed him.

"Why don't you use our name when you sing?" I said, hoisting up the big amp.

He shuffled it tight against the guitar cases, to keep them from moving. I was holding my breath.

"It's no big deal," he said finally. "Mom never

talks about her family — I don't know what their fight was about — but I think she misses them."

He jumped back onto the ground. "I just thought if maybe they heard their name, heard it like it was famous, they'd wonder. And maybe look for us, or be proud."

I was proud. I grabbed him suddenly around the shoulders in a hug.

"What was that for?" Daniel said, surprised.

"Because I don't do cards," I said.

As we walked the highway back to The Pas, I wondered if he was the older brother and I had just been born first.

We went to the cafe beside Rene's Guitar Bar. From the cubicle in the entrance I made my first phone call, to have the truck towed in. I hadn't noticed any damage but I wanted them to check anyway, once they got it to the garage. It's the stuff you can't see, like a bent frame, that can give you the most trouble.

By the time I got back to the little window booth, Daniel had ordered breakfast. Two tall glasses, one orange juice and one water, were waiting for me. Everything ached. My joints felt like bones grinding into bones. But there's no quick fix for a hangover. Just time and liquids, and maybe aspirin.

I drank the water, and then the juice. Daniel's order came, one of those country breakfast specials – eggs and ham and hash browns, toast on the side. I was amazed to see that much food in front of him, but I remembered he hadn't eaten at all yesterday.

He was grinning at me. "You look like hell."

"Thanks. Feel it, too."

"You want something?"

I shook my head. "I have to phone Dad."

"Yeah, you do," he said as he began to cut up his fruit.

I got change from the cashier. Right up until I dialed, I didn't know which number I was going to punch in first.

"Good morning, Five Star Ford," Judi said brightly.

"Judi, this is Jens."

Her voice dropped. "I'll put you right through to Mr. Lahanni."

The line never rang, not even once. His deep voice was suddenly against my ear. "Jens, where's my truck?"

"It's here with me in The Pas."

"Is it all right? Are you?"

I hesitated. "It's...getting checked out. There was a storm and I wound up in the ditch."

"If it's driveable, just bring it in. Any work we'll do in our shop."

"I'll pay for it —"

"Yes, you will." He hesitated. "Jens, I want

you to know, you were about two hours away from being charged with theft. I was giving you until noon."

I felt dizzy again, a pulse of nausea. I could see how close I'd been to the edge.

"Maybe you think I'm being a hardass, but I like you, Jens," Jack continued. "If I covered for you, you might get out too far." I heard him sigh. "Believe me, that doesn't help anybody."

"Thank you, Mr. Lahanni," I said.

I hung up and for a moment I just stood there, breathing. I had nothing to prop me up now, no big win to push me through. It was just me.

My father answered.

"Jens. My God, where are you? Where's Daniel? We heard about the storm."

I told him we'd made it to The Pas, and that I'd put the truck in the ditch. No one was going to take the blame for that except me.

"Were you drinking?"

"Yes," I said softly. I didn't know how he knew. There was a silence that I just had to live through, hanging onto the phone, feeling small. My father didn't help me. He only waited.

"Dad, I screwed up so bad," I blurted at last.

I ran out of change. He had to phone me back. But I stuck it out and stayed there and I told him, even about Daniel and the tapes.

Maybe I was getting us both in trouble but the problem with being honest is that once you start, it's such a relief you don't want to stop.

"What are you going to do now, son?" he said finally. No pressure but I could feel him beside me, as if he was standing right there.

"I...think I need to come home."

His breath rushed out. A sigh seemed to squeeze me around the shoulders. "Thank God."

We talked for a minute more, about where he would meet us in Winnipeg, and when.

"Okay, see you tonight." I hesitated. "Give my love to Mom."

I walked back to the table a lot lighter. I might never know for sure if he was my real dad. But I knew how I felt, and that was real.

Daniel had not only finished his meal, he'd started a piece of pie. I laughed out loud. "Who could eat banana cream for breakfast?"

"You," he said, sliding the plate toward me.

I looked at it. Home made, with real whipped cream, but I wasn't hungry that way. I pushed the plate back at him.

"Buck up. You're building a garage this summer."

He rolled his eyes. It made me smile, I'm not even sure why. Maybe because I'd known he'd do it.

"I'd better have some toast," I said, signaling

for the waitress. "I'm building a garage, too."

We walked the four blocks to the autobody place, jumping over puddles all the way. I still couldn't believe how the weather had turned. The sun lit up windows and flashed on the cars as they passed us. There hadn't been time to sand the streets. The Pas seemed to emerge wet and clean under our feet.

Daniel was watching the sidewalk, maybe so he wouldn't walk through water.

"Tell me again," he said, "everything Kruse told you."

I did, feeling a flutter between my ribs. In the daylight, it was exciting news.

"Home Grown is small but they're real," I finished. "Think about it. You're only sixteen. Who knows where this could go?"

He nodded absently. I threw up my hands.

"Daniel, you should be doing cartwheels! What's the matter with you?"

"I don't like him, Jens. The guy's...a weasel."

I knew that for a fact, but telling Daniel wouldn't help him at this point.

"He's what you've got," I said. "He's the one who set up the deal. You've got to watch out, that's all. Read the contract. Ask questions, and listen to the answers. Talk to other musicians, or write in to those magazines you read all the time. Find out what's fair. This is your future," I continued. "You've got to do the research."

He turned abruptly. "Why don't you be my agent?"

I stopped, too. Moments from the last three days seemed to leap back at me: flashing his tape in Starling, standing on my truck hood in Easton, handing out guitar picks – and getting them back. He'd been right that day. I did love it.

"Because you're the best new guitarist in the province and you deserve better than me," I said. "I'm...a kid, Daniel. I don't even know what I don't know."

He opened his mouth and then shut it.

"Besides," I said, starting to walk again, "I'm going back to school. We both are."

For a minute there was only the sloshing sound as we tramped through a melting drift. Neither one of us would get out of this with dry feet.

"But could you help me figure out what to ask?" he said finally.

"Sure."

"And be there for the answers?" he said.

"Well, yeah. That's the interesting part."

"Okay." Daniel was smiling to himself. My brother knew me.

The truck's front bumper had been pushed in and the oil pan was dented, but it'd make it back to the city.

"Well, then you just owe me for the tow," the mechanic said to me, adding up the taxes on a calculator. Daniel had his wallet open before the total, and he counted out the money almost proudly. He liked paying his own way. It reminded me that I'd liked it, too.

I debated with myself as we walked out to the truck. I knew I could make an arrangement with the Five Star shop, whatever I wound up owing for repairs. But Mr. Delbeggio had to be dealt with as soon as possible. I took a breath.

"Daniel —" I started.

"Okay. How much?"

I laughed with relief. "You're way too easy with your money."

"Not really. I'm charging you seven percent on it."

"You shark!" I gave him a friendly shove. "Don't I get a family rate?"

"That is the family rate," he said, grinning.

What was left of the storm was drifted in the ditch, or gathered in the brush; I had a feeling it would be gone by afternoon. The highway was clear and almost dry, and I was glad to be on it. I couldn't make this drive fast enough. But as we passed the city limits, I asked, "You want to stop in Easton?"

Daniel shook his head no.

"I hope your Rosetown bootleg isn't going to

get rich over this," I said carefully.

He looked at me. With two days' stubble on his face and clothes he'd slept in, he looked rough. We both did.

"You can talk to people, Jens. You don't know what it's like..."

"To what? Be lonely?"

"Yeah."

"Right. And I've got a great job and my own apartment and a new truck, too." I sighed. "Just because I can talk to strangers doesn't make me a good...friend to anybody. Nobody dates me twice," I admitted quietly.

My eyes were on the road but I could feel him watching me. I'd spent a lot of time building that myth, too. Maybe all I could do was start again at the beginning. An idea came to me and I felt my face flush. The steering wheel was slippery under my hands. I hadn't been nervous like this in a long time.

"I was thinking maybe this summer I'd phone up Mona Perenthaler," I said.

"To go out?"

I grinned. "No. To sell her a car."

Daniel's hat was on the seat between us and he picked it up, started playing with it, flipping it over and over in his hands.

"Chantel said we should write, so that's what I'm going to do — write." There was an odd slant in his voice, thoughtful but determined. "I figure yesterday was worth three, four songs, easy."

My shoulders relaxed, as if I'd put down something heavy. "I understand you need a guitar for that," I said.

He turned abruptly, his eyes lit up.

"Can we make it to Mickey's before they close?"

"Oh, maybe," I said, squeezing the accelerator. I'd let Daniel down a lot of times, but this wasn't going to be one of them.

I felt the familiar kick under my ribs as the truck surged forward, pushing the speed limit, nudging over it, the road and sky calling me to run. Maybe I would always love this — having somewhere to go and a reason to get there. I couldn't believe it was a bad thing. It all depended on where I was headed, and who I took with me.

I suddenly had to know.

"What's your favorite ice cream?"

Daniel looked at me as if I was crazy. "What? Why?"

"Come on, just tell me."

He thought about it for a second. "Orange sherbet. Why?"

"Just wondering," I said. "Mine's Rocky Road."

Acknowledgments

I would like to thank Dan Frechette, a very talented young guitarist, singer and songwriter who generously shared his experiences and insight.

I would also like to thank Big Dave McLean and Gord Kidder, the original Blues Brats, who really did open for Muddy Waters in Winnipeg in 1977. Renowned blues artists, they didn't need the help of my fictional character, Bourbon Ray.

Get inside the author's mind – books,
background, point of view.
Connect with Diana Wieler at:
www.makersgallery.com/wieler/